Journeys to Peace

"Parables of Love, Forgiveness, and Grace"

TR Brennan

Copyright © 2022 TR Brennan.

All rights reserved. No part of this book may be used or reproduced by any means, graphic, electronic, or mechanical, including photocopying, recording, taping or by any information storage retrieval system without the written permission of the author except in the case of brief quotations embodied in critical articles and reviews.

This is a work of fiction. All of the characters, names, incidents, organizations, and dialogue in this novel are either the products of the author's imagination or are used fictitiously.

LifeRich Publishing is a registered trademark of The Reader's Digest Association, Inc.

LifeRich Publishing books may be ordered through booksellers or by contacting:

LifeRich Publishing
1663 Liberty Drive
Bloomington, IN 47403
www.liferichpublishing.com
844-686-9607

Because of the dynamic nature of the Internet, any web addresses or links contained in this book may have changed since publication and may no longer be valid. The views expressed in this work are solely those of the author and do not necessarily reflect the views of the publisher, and the publisher hereby disclaims any responsibility for them.

Any people depicted in stock imagery provided by Getty Images are models, and such images are being used for illustrative purposes only.
Certain stock imagery © Getty Images.

Holy Bible, New International Version®, NIV® Copyright ©1973, 1978, 1984, 2011 by Biblica, Inc.® Used by permission. All rights reserved worldwide.

Copyright © 1993, 2002, 2018 by Eugene H. Peterson

Holy Bible, New Living Translation, copyright © 1996, 2004, 2015 by Tyndale House Foundation. Used by permission of Tyndale House Publishers, Inc., Carol Stream, Illinois 60188. All rights reserved.

ISBN: 978-1-4897-3973-5 (sc)
ISBN: 978-1-4897-3971-1 (hc)
ISBN: 978-1-4897-3972-8 (e)

Library of Congress Control Number: 2021925459

Print information available on the last page.

LifeRich Publishing rev. date: 01/19/2022

This book is dedicated to

God, the Father of Creation; His Son, Yeshua; and the Holy Spirit.

To First Nations people across the world, who journeyed before us and endured hardships and death brought on by hate and greed; for that, I am deeply sorry.

And to all people—no matter race, color, or creed—who are hurting, lonely, sick, depressed, and fearful; may you find the Way Maker, Jesus Christ, for He will guide you through your journeys in life to peace.

"But I will restore you to health
and heal your wounds," declares the Lord.

—Jeremiah 30:17 (NIV)

CONTENTS

Preface xiii

A PARABLE OF LOVE

Chapter 1 : The Cabin 1
Chapter 2 : Meeting Mr. Castleman 5
Chapter 3 : My Story 9
Chapter 4 : My Journey Begins 13
Chapter 5 : Healing My Broken Life 17
Chapter 6 : A Deeper Walk 21
Chapter 7 : The Ultimate Gift of Love 25
Chapter 8 : The Day 29
Chapter 9 : Epilogue—Open Your Hearts 33

A PARABLE OF FORGIVENESS

Chapter 1 : Walking the Jesus Way 39
Chapter 2 : Remembering My Past 43
Chapter 3 : Journey to My People 47
Chapter 4 : Reconnecting 53
Chapter 5 : Building Bridges of Trust 57
Chapter 6 : The Ultimate Gift of Forgiveness 63
Chapter 7 : A Stranger in Town 67
Chapter 8 : Reconciliation 73
Chapter 9 : Epilogue—Arise, My People 79

A PARABLE OF GRACE

Chapter 1 : Retreat to the Mountains. 87
Chapter 2 : Refinement in the Fire 93
Chapter 3 : Escape to the Hills 99
Chapter 4 : Perseverance 103
Chapter 5 : Tragedy Strikes. 109
Chapter 6 : The Ultimate Gift of Grace 113
Chapter 7 : Restoration. 117
Chapter 8 : A Great Awakening. 123
Chapter 9 : Epilogue—Will You Be Ready?. 131

Bibliography 135
Afterword. 137
Let All Things Praise Him 139
About the Author. 141

A special thank you to the following:

Yahweh, Yeshua, and Holy Spirit for inspiration, wisdom,
and guidance to complete this God assignment.

Jamie, my husband, who supports me with
unconditional love and godly prayers.

Our daughter Jennifer, our miracle from God,
who continually brings laughter
and joy into our lives. And most especially for using her
God-given editing talents to make this a book of excellence.

My parents who continually love and support their children.

My cherished sister Heidi, who always supported my dreams
and will be forever in my heart.

Our dear friends Barry and Luanne, who have taught us so much about
their native culture and the love of Yah—Jesus Christ.

A special thank you to First Nation believers, who
are paving a path to a great spiritual awakening.

PREFACE

This book consists of three separate parables that can be read independently, each distinct from the others; therefore, the beginning of each tale has a short recap for clarity. The intent was to write easy-reading parables to encourage others to ponder love, forgiveness, and grace; however, they can also be read consecutively.

Journeys to Peace is written through the eyes of a Native American, a First Nation woman; the intention isn't to appropriate or dishonor First Nation people but to honor and educate non-natives to the horrific injustices they suffered in the past and issues they still face today. This book is for every culture, race, color, or creed as an encouragement to find unconditional love and forgiveness while learning about the grace of God.

Though fictional, this book incorporates personal experiences. It is for believers and nonbelievers and can be used as an evangelical tool to learn about God, Jesus, and the Holy Spirit. It also shares information on how to receive Jesus (Yeshua) as one's Savior and incorporates teachings on the body, soul, spirit, and unity.

Finally, it teaches that to live an abundant life, we must watch thoughts and words spoken, align them to the Word of God through prayer and thanksgiving, meditate in the Word daily, and live according to the Spirit of God within.

I pray these parables will bless you.

A PARABLE OF LOVE

Dear Children,

For those who are lonely, fearful, and in despair, may this parable of love lift your spirits, heal your soul, and bring new hope to you.

May you be renewed with a desire to live life to the fullest and accomplish what God the Father ordained for you.

You are His unique creation, and you are loved.

God's blessings and peace ~

CHAPTER 1

The Cabin

I fondly remember Mr. Bob Castleman. He was a gentle, compassionate man. He was a good man, a godly man. He cared about people and had a heart of grace like none other. His only purpose in life was to serve God and love His people—unknown to most. He accomplished this mission through his ministry, which was his life.

I met him long ago during the most challenging time of my life. I had everything but felt like I had nothing. I was alone with no hope, joy, or desire to continue living in the empty void people call "life." It was Mr. Castleman who turned my life around. He taught me about faith, hope, and the unconditional love of our Savior.

Mr. Castleman lived a simple life with minimal needs. He lived in a small cabin on the outskirts of a little town in New Hampshire. To get to the cabin, I had to carefully cross a wooden plank bridge over a brook. As I stepped, peering through the cracks underfoot, I could see the water rushing over stones and massive rocks. I could feel the water splash up onto my feet, as though being baptized by Creator God Himself.

The lush forest that hid the bridge leading to the cabin's north entrance created a green canopy. Maples, mighty oaks, white birches, and pines intertwined with colors and majesty. It felt as though I were entering a sacred place adorned by creation made just for me.

The cabin was modest but livable. One large room contained a sitting area, a kitchen, a small table, and an attached sunroom. In one corner, the small bathroom had an eco-friendly peat moss toilet and a large claw-foot tub that he would fill with buckets of warm water when it was time to bathe. The walls were adorned with pine boards, which created a friendly and peaceful atmosphere I could feel as soon as I entered. Under the window benches were bookshelves filled to capacity, though the only book I'd ever seen him read was the Bible.

Mr. Castleman had no need for a regular bed; he slept peacefully and soundly, wrapped in the weaving of his Mayan hammock. He compared it to the cradling of a mother's womb or being covered in the arms of His loving Father.

Across the room was a small cassette player, which quietly filled the room with the sounds of native flute and nature music. "Tsa'ne Dos'e played one of the best versions of 'Amazing Grace' I have ever heard," Mr. Castleman told me one day.

The room smelled of herbs, spices, and essential oils—gifts from the earth provided by Father God. In sight were various gemstones such as amethyst, pyrite, rose quartz, citrine, turquoise, and celestite—to name a few. They weren't used for rituals as some have taught and corrupted; they were just reminders of the beauty and creation of God's handiwork.

One stone, in particular, looked like a big rock, but inside were beautiful white crystals that had formed. Mr. Castleman used the rock to show how we look on the outside compared to the beauty God sees created on the inside.

The cabin was situated high on a hill, evidenced by the shortness of breath visitors experienced while hiking up to the wooden bridge. To the east, just beyond roughly an acre of woods, one could see the beating of massive ocean waves, which had carved out bluffs the Creator had uniquely designed.

To the west, at the foot of a steep bank, one could see a pond that was continuously filled by fresh spring water. The pond was surrounded by cattails dancing ever so slightly in the wind. The water was stocked with bullheads and goldfish. It always amused me when Mr. Castleman brought out some fish food and called the fish to eat. Each time, they obediently came to the surface and gobbled everything in sight.

The pond was adorned with pink and white lily pads, where one could often see the herons enjoying a fish dinner. Around the edges of the pond were three benches in different areas. There was a beautiful, purple bee balm bush next to one seat, and if I sat quietly long enough, a hummingbird stopped by for a drink of sweet nectar.

Another bench was under a willow tree, where the birds stopped by and sang me a song. The third bench sat directly in the sun and moonlight, where nothing was hidden in the shadows, and the warmth of the sun was like a hug from Creator God. Beyond the pond—in the far distance—was flattened land as far as the eye could see, filled with wildflowers, bobolinks, swooping and gliding swallows, deer, coyotes, and an occasional fox.

On the south side of the cabin, the woods were dense, and the air was filled with a pine scent. The woods were alive with song and activity from chickadees, veeries, pileated woodpeckers, squirrels, chipmunks, and a nightly hoot from a barred owl. Under the largest tree, a white pine, there was a bench where I could sit and rest my head on the massive trunk. Stories of the ancient tree were endless, always giving glory to God. It was never worshipped, as some have claimed.

In every direction, there were meditative areas, where one could sit and talk to God. Each site was unique, but all helped heal past hurts, as I would later learn from Mr. Castleman.

CHAPTER 2

Meeting Mr. Castleman

The day I met Mr. Castleman, I knew my life would never be the same. His piercing eyes reflected a light I had never seen before, a light that drew me in. His voice was gentle, kind, and peaceful yet commanding—one that could calm a storm. He walked into my life with an oversized, down under leather hat and a smile that would have melted anyone's heart. A simple man, he wore jeans, a jean jacket, work boots, and carried a backpack.

Mr. Castleman was the kind of person who caused one to think, *This must be what Jesus is like.* He exuded such love and peace that one wanted to sit, listen, and talk to him for hours. I was befuddled yet intrigued. Something about him was different, seemingly almost inhuman, yet he was standing right in front of me.

After a short conversation, he told me God had sent him to come and see me. Startled and alarmed, I instinctively backed away. He continued to speak in reassuring tones, saying he was there to help. Without saying a word, I knew he could see deep into my soul. I was exposed, frightened, and at peace—all at the same moment.

He shared with me that he had spent years studying medicinal plants and the Word of God. I could tell from his demeanor that he was confident and at peace with who he was, which I immediately envied. Not much more was said after that initial greeting, and he soon said goodbye.

At the time, I owned and operated a small bookshop called Journeys, located in Graceville, a small coastal town in New Hampshire with a population of less than a thousand. The bookstore was barely thriving, and with the introduction of the mega bookstores, I knew it was just a matter of time before Journeys would close.

Journeys was quaint and before its time. It had sitting areas with overstuffed chairs for reading, small café-style tables, and chairs for sipping coffee or tea. Customers could hear the trickle of water from a fountain I had made out of rocks, adding another level of tranquility to the atmosphere.

A local bakery provided muffins, scones, and a selection of cookies; and the aromas filled the air, reminding me of home. The warmth, peace, and camaraderie allowed patrons to slip away for a time into another world, forgetting the hustle and bustle of time-crunched commitments.

On occasion, Journeys hosted mic night for a taste of "coffeehouse music," and at times, an author stopped by for a signing. The book selections were mostly nonfiction and self-help, with some fiction and a few Bibles scattered here and there. Relaxing music, available for purchase, played throughout the day. I also sold gift cards, knickknacks, and puzzles. I loved my little shop. Just like the patrons, I was able to block out the world once I was inside.

After Mr. Castleman left, I started cleaning up, preparing to close shop for the day. I then noticed a small white card, what looked like a business card, sitting on one of the shelves. Perplexed, I picked it up. It simply said, "B. C.," followed by what appeared to be a phone number. Not giving it much thought, I set it on the back counter, still thinking, *That was all a bit weird.*

Journeys was nestled on Main Street in the middle of town, alongside other mom-and-pop shops. Though the buildings were connected on each side, they were each unique in color and design. They stood, akin to the style of the Victorian painted ladies, only one-quarter of the size.

On either side of Journeys, the shops were active with customers. To my right was a florist, and to my left was an arts and crafts shop. Graceville was self-reliant with its own grocery center, dry cleaners, liquor store, bakery, bar, and my personal favorite, the Corner Diner.

I was always amazed that there were churches of so many denominations in our little town—Roman Catholic, Methodist, Baptist, Full Gospel, Pentecostal, and even a Jewish synagogue. Given Graceville's small population, it seemed there were more places to worship than there were people, and each denomination claimed to be the "one, true way." I made it a point to stay away from them; to me they had God in a box, and the likes of me would never be accepted.

Throughout the next few weeks, I saw Mr. Castleman walking around town. Sometimes he carried a grocery sack; other times he just passed through with a walking stick. My curiosity was piqued; I began asking around town whether anyone knew who he was. Most shrugged, stating he was quiet, kept to himself, lived to the north of town up on the hill, and walked everywhere he went. The consensus was that he was an inexplicable stranger, mysterious and eccentric, so people avoided him yet oddly knew enough to gossip about him.

CHAPTER 3

My Story

I was born and raised on a reservation in northern North Dakota in a small community, home to the Ojibway people. I couldn't wait to leave and get away from the injustices and poverty of my people. Nothing seemed to change day after day, year after year. The Ojibway people were poor, undereducated, and depressed—no fault of their own. They lived in hopelessness, desperation, and third-world conditions. I watched my parents struggle to provide for us, the odds stacked against them. Drinking became the norm to numb life's dealings, suicide was an escape for others, and drugs were rampant. In these conditions, loneliness and despair become too much to bear.

You cannot blame my brothers and sisters for their choices; our trust was broken many times. They were isolated people. They didn't belong in the "white man's world," nor in the one the government had created for them. My native relatives were the only people who didn't have a choice, a country, or a place to call home.

Hopelessness is an epidemic. I was determined to leave as soon as I could. I worked many long hours, finding any odd jobs that would bring in some money. I stashed away money each time I could, but most of it went to help support my family. I didn't finish high school because the building was in disrepair, teachers and supplies were lacking, and in reality, no one really cared. Neither did I. Fortunately, I always had a voracious desire to read, which helped me pursue work and escape into a different world, leaving depression far from my thoughts.

As the living conditions worsened, the already disturbingly high suicide rates increased rapidly. I watched in horror as another one was reported—this time a twelve-year-old boy who had lived on the reservation down the road from me. I went to school with his sister; it was heartbreaking to imagine what she was going through. I saw my peers huffing gas, doing drugs, and drinking until they passed out to ease their pain. If I didn't leave, I knew I would join the ranks of them.

In my early twenties, I saw an opportunity to get out and took it. One of my cousins was fortunate to break out of this vicious cycle by acquiring a scholarship to a college, a rare feat. I convinced her to let me tag along. My only goal was to get out and never go back. I didn't care where I was going as long as I got out. I prepared, gathering all the money I had. I left, hoping never to look back on that life again.

My cousin's school was on the East Coast in Massachusetts, so I asked her to drop me off at the local bus station. My heart's desire had always been to see the ocean, so I headed to New Hampshire. Upon arriving, I found an ad in the local newspaper; someone was looking for a clerk in a small bookshop. I think back now and thank God that my persistent and tenacious personality provided well for me. When I set my mind to do something, it remains set until I accomplish it.

I was in awe of my new surroundings. With Graceville being such a small town, I quickly found the bookshop, Journeys, and met the owner, Mrs. Gregory. She was a sweet, elderly lady with silver hair and the bluest eyes I had ever seen. She was a widow and had never had any children. She welcomed me with open arms, even with my dark complexion and jet-black eyes and hair.

She had a small room above the bookshop and offered me room and board as long as I helped her run the bookshop. For me, it was a miracle! I quickly settled into my new life, learning every aspect of running a small bookshop. I remained somewhat secluded and wary of people. I slowly warmed up, but I always made sure my wall of protection was up and intact. I didn't talk about my past, and no one inquired, seeing that I was different. Fear on both sides, I guess.

Life was pretty good for a few years. I learned all I could, and Mrs.

Gregory became my family. She tried to talk to me about my past, but I was determined to live life with no thoughts about my family, the reservation, or the past life I'd left behind. Mrs. Gregory respected that; however, I could see the pain in her eyes. She had come to love me as her own, and her heart broke because she wasn't able to help me.

Soon that dreaded day came: Mrs. Gregory unexpectedly passed away. I was devastated—alone and unsure of my future, the only family I had known here gone in the blink of an eye. Not long after, a lawyer entered the bookshop and said he needed to talk to me. Shaken and flustered, I sat down, figuring he was putting the shop up for sale, and I had to get out. To my surprise, it was the opposite. Mrs. Gregory had named me as her sole survivor and willed Journeys to me as well as the funds she had saved. I sat there, stunned, tears in my eyes, saying nothing. The lawyer kept asking whether I was all right.

Finally coming to my senses, I replied, "Yes, just shocked."

I managed the shop well enough, but the loneliness and heartache from missing her were at times overwhelming. I had no one. Realizing I could now lose Journeys too because the big corporate bookstores were taking over the market was more than I could handle. I went through my days numb. A few patrons tried to reach out to me but to no avail. A few good-intentioned Christians approached me but basically pushed me further away with their threats that I was going to hell because I didn't know their Jesus.

I thought many times of just running away like I had from the reservation, but what would I do? Where would I go? I had a fleeting thought of contacting my family but knew that would only seal the deal on life for me. Putting my head down on my arms in despair, I saw a card slightly sticking out from under the register. I pulled it out and saw the letters "B. C." scrawled on a business card, now faded.

I was puzzling over this discovery when suddenly my head shot up when I realized B. C. stood for Bob Castleman. I thought how strange it was that I had found this card; it had been almost a year since I talked with Mr. Castleman. How bizarre was that!

CHAPTER 4

My Journey Begins

Just when I thought things couldn't get worse, a few days later I had extreme pain in my leg and went to urgent care. The doctor informed me that I had a blood clot. He continued, "Good news, though. It's not a deep vein clot, only a surface blood clot. But if it's not better in three to four days, we'll have to operate." I limped back to the shop, more discouraged than ever. I had no medical insurance, and this would surely destroy me.

With the B. C. card in hand, I remembered Mr. Castleman saying he studied medicinal herbs. I knew from my upbringing that herbs and plants had many healing properties, but that was all I knew. I then did the unthinkable, something entirely unlike myself. Not knowing whether he was still in the area, I picked up the phone and dialed, holding my breath.

Mr. Castleman answered, as kind and gracious as I remembered. Desperate for help, I promptly told him about the clot in my leg. He said he remembered me and suggested I wrap my leg with pieces of wilted cabbage. "Wilt them in the microwave or on top of the stove, but be careful they aren't too hot," he instructed. "Then put the leaves on your leg and wrap your leg with an ace bandage or vet wrap."

He said he would stop in and check on me in a few days. To my surprise, Mr. Castleman actually stopped by. I shared with him that the pain had subsided within twenty minutes, and I felt something funny in my leg. I took off the wrap to find the blood clot had burst, and the pain was gone by the next day, leaving nothing more than a nasty-looking bruise.

From that moment on, Mr. Castleman became my mentor, teacher, and friend. He would lead me into a new, wonderful world—a place of love, healing, and forgiveness. Thankfully, the process was slow, and he took extra care not to overstep boundaries because he knew that move would frighten me off.

He would stop by the shop for a while to say hello, and we chatted about everyday things. One day when he stopped, he invited me to come for a visit sometime to his cabin. He talked about it with such admiration that it enticed me to step out of my safety zone.

One would think that a woman wouldn't go to a cabin alone with an older man, but there was an inexplicable peace and comfort with Mr. Castleman after all our talks; I felt as if I knew him. I also found self-assurance since I had been a fighter back in the day.

On the reservation—or, as some would call it, "the Rez"—men often took advantage of native women. I knew how to fight because the government, police, and Rez security officers either didn't care or were "too busy" to intervene. Most of us girls learned how to protect ourselves simply because we had to. Sadly, some women lost the battle and sometimes their lives through abuse or random abductions—atrocities that are still happening today.

I will never forget the day when I first visited Mr. Castleman. His directions were clear and succinct, and I found myself entering a long, winding path that led me up a steep hill to a wooden bridge. I carefully stepped across the planks as I noticed the rushing brook flowing underneath. Leery of everything, I moved forward, stepping slowly to avoid tripping or falling. One would think, being of native heritage, that I would have knowledge of the woods; however, it was desolate where we lived. There was nothing but dry land that couldn't produce a crop if life depended on it.

Mr. Castleman was waiting at the end of the path, standing before a unique, beautiful little cabin. Instead of taking me inside, he said, "Let's stroll through the woods." He wanted to show me his pond, which would soon become a favorite spot of mine. Mr. Castleman began talking to me about God, the Creator of the world, and all He has done for us. At the first mention of religion, I immediately put up my defenses, wondering how the Creator I knew could allow us to be pushed to reservations and live in such inhumane circumstances. Mr. Castleman, noticing I was becoming withdrawn, decided to take another approach.

He then began telling me about native teachings he had learned while traveling the world. He explained that most native cultures believed the cardinal directions consisted of different earthly elements. Being so far removed from my customs and traditions intrigued me to learn what other cultures taught. I asked him to tell me more, feeling this was a safe subject.

We headed farther west and came upon this beautiful pond. The water was peaceful and serene; in fact, it reflected what I saw in Mr. Castleman. He was calm, slow, and steady in his talk, filled with unconditional love. I clearly saw the love he had for God, a God I had never known. He called God "Abba" (which means "Father") quite often. He explained there are many names for God, such as Creator, Yahweh, and Lord, but his favorite was Abba.

We sat on a bench and continued to discuss the four directions God had created and how powerful and loving God was. I brought the conversation back to my comfort zone and asked about what the native's view of the west was. Mr. Castleman said some believed the west's element was water, and through listening and silence, one became "The Way of the Teacher—one who shares wisdom."[1]

He continued by saying that silently sitting by water helped heal the soul when a person was in turmoil in life. He also added that different types of water aided in different situations. If you were quiet and listened to the small voice inside, he said, God would guide you as to which type of water you needed. It could be a babbling brook; a still, calm pond; a waterfall; or the majesty of the ocean—God would direct you if you asked.

I listened and didn't say a word. The only thing I knew was that, sitting at the pond, I felt what must have been peace for the first time in my life. Mr. Castleman told me that past hurts, fears, shame, and regrets all needed to be dealt with to find inner peace and heal the soul.

He further explained that God had created people with a soul. The

---

[1] Angeles Arrien, *The Four-Fold Way – Walking the Paths of the Warrior, Teacher, Healer and Visionary*, (New York: HarperCollins, 1997), 107.

soul is where your emotions are, your source of feelings, your mind, and your thoughts. He said that if I had past issues I needed to work through, hitting two sticks together would help release the anger and break the past cycle. I was intrigued. That was the first of many meetings to come.

As I left, Mr. Castleman said I could stop by anytime to sit at the pond. Before I left, he blessed me with two beautiful wooden sticks I could use for some soul work. The sticks were wrapped in leather strips on one end and had beautiful feathers hanging from them along with some beads. I graciously accepted them and headed home, thinking that no way would I use those sticks.

CHAPTER 5

Healing My Broken Life

A few days later, Journeys' sales continued to drop, becoming a more significant concern. Anxiety and fears crept in, and I saw the wooden sticks lying on the counter. With no customers and nothing else to do, I picked up the sticks and started hitting them together. To my surprise, doing so felt good. With so much pent-up emotion and frustration, I hit them harder and harder. Mr. Castleman had said hitting the sticks together would help break past issues—anger, regrets, and pain—and I had to admit that the sticks really helped! My anxiety subsided, and I even thought for a split second, *I might be able to leave all my problems to Mr. Castleman's God.* Wow, where did that come from? In no way would I trust someone I couldn't see.

My lessons continued with Mr. Castleman. He taught me so much. We walked through a thicket of woods east of the cabin and ventured upon a cliff overlooking the ocean. From this view, the sea appeared like a massive body of water. The power of the waves hitting the sides of the mountain made impressions I can only liken to artwork. I noticed a fire pit with benches around it; Mr. Castleman had told me that some native people attributed the fire to the east, which makes sense with the sun rising in the east. I was beginning to see that this God was creative, powerful, and everywhere if I would just open my eyes and heart.

We sat around the fire many evenings, talking about God's creation, all of it—mankind, animals, nature, earth, water, wind, and fire. Mr. Castleman shared that some native cultures believed the east direction was "The Way of the Visionary."[2] Walking with bells, singing, and meditating on the Word brings vision to one's life. It was certainly something to ponder. Mr. Castleman had such a way with words that my heart began to soften, and I found myself wanting to hear more about his God. He told me, "Soon, very soon, you will be ready to hear about the greatest love story there ever was."

I found that with the walks we took, our talks by the fire, and time sitting by the pond, a change had taken place deep in my soul. My emotions were shifting. The peace I had been feeling was increasing, and this was a whole new experience for me.

One of our walks was behind the south side of Mr. Castleman's cabin, an area thick with woods. He shared that south represented the earth; lying on the ground, drumming, and storytelling were "The Way of the Healer."[3] As we walked and talked, the ground was fragrant with the smell of pines. I felt the coolness of the woods and heard the birds singing with joy. Mr. Castleman had a bench near a giant white pine, and he told me the story of how the white pine was significant to the Native American Haudenosaunee; it was the tree of peace. Each bunch of needles had five needles, which represented the uniting of five warring nations—Mohawk, Oneida, Onondaga, Cayuga, and Seneca. Later, Tuscarora was added, and all are now governed by the Six Nations Council of the Iroquois Confederacy.

As we walked, Mr. Castleman shared stories about medicinal plants found throughout the woods and fields. He told me his favorite plant was mullein, an excellent plant for helping with congestion. He said, "You can dry and steep the leaves to make a tea or smoke them." I was again amazed by what could be found in nature. Maybe hearing about this God or Creator, as some called Him, wasn't as threatening as I had first thought. If nothing else, the matter had already proved to be thought provoking.

Sitting by that great tree, Mr. Castleman gave me a gift wrapped in a piece of cloth. Slowly opening it, I was amazed by the colors and patterns. I

---

[2] Angeles Arrien, 77.
[3] Angeles Arrien, 47.

had seen something like this on the Rez but ironically had never taken the time to learn what it was. Mr. Castleman gracefully explained that it was a wampum—made of tiny, cylindrical quahog shell beads strung together. "In your native culture, it can be worn as a decorative belt, and in the past, it was used for sending messages and recording peace treaties, pledges, and marriages. It was even used as an exchange for money."

Attached to the wampum was a small pocket knife, the most beautiful knife I had ever seen. Mr. Castleman taught me how to whittle a stick into different shapes. I couldn't believe how great it felt just to be carving, touching wood, admiring the grain, and wondering what the final creation would be. Interestingly enough, it was almost reflective of the transformation happening within me.

As we continued to sit, Mr. Castleman gently encouraged me to talk about my past. "It was time to heal," he told me. "It is time to let go of the past, forgive, and reconnect with your family." I respected his opinion but was reluctant to follow his advice. Knowing my heart, he suggested that I do some "drum work."

What an odd thing to say, I thought.

On my next visit, Mr. Castleman brought out a deer hide that had been prepared with non-iodized salt and then soaked in water. He showed me how to scrape the hide, remove the hair, and stretch it over a round wooden frame. We then made holes in the edges of the hide with a hammer and dole, and pulled the hide around the frame. We also took some strips of hide we had cut, which looked like laces. I held a round metal ring on the back of the drum so Mr. Castleman could weave the laces through the holes to the ring. He then pulled the hide tight until there was no give left. Then he said, "That's it for today. Time for the hide and lace to dry. Please come back in a few days."

Over the next few days, my anticipation grew considerably—so much so that when it came time to visit again, I ran up the steep hill to Mr. Castleman's cabin. I was so excited, and seeing the drum was beyond my expectations. It had the most beautiful deep, resonant sound. Mr. Castleman then showed me how to color it using Kool-Aid. I chose red and called it my "fire drum."

To my surprise, Mr. Castleman was right; I did much healing heart work with that drum. It awakened deep within me a heartbeat of life, and I felt more alive than I had ever felt before. As I continued my drum work, I realized I suddenly started to find hope for what had once been a hopeless future.

CHAPTER 6

A Deeper Walk

The seasons flew by, and Journeys was still hanging on by a thread. I started to offer some classes on the things I had learned from Mr. Castleman, bringing in some new business. As I headed up the hill to the cabin, I stopped and noticed the air—how wonderful it was. I began dancing with joy and picked up some pebbles to shake with my hands cupped together. The rattle sound was beautiful. I felt as if I were mighty, ready to face the world and all it had to offer.

I told Mr. Castleman about this when I arrived at the cabin, and he smiled with his eyes. He said, "You see, you have heard that still, quiet voice of God within you. He has whispered the meaning of the final direction, which we have yet to discuss." Mr. Castleman continued, "You see, all that you mentioned are attributes natives relate to the north direction—the air, standing, rattle, and dancing are 'The Way of the Warrior.'"[4] I was speechless yet beaming inside.

Mr. Castleman then invited me into his cabin. I had been inside before, but I'd never stayed long. This time he asked me to sit in a big wicker chair by his reading shelf. I gazed around his tiny space in awe of the items before me and the peace I felt there—much like how I imagine heaven to be.

---

[4] Angeles Arrien, 13.

Mr. Castleman first put his sun conure parrot, Hadassah, back in her cage, for he allowed her to wander around the house until he had visitors. Hadassah had vibrant golden-yellow plumage with orange underparts on her face. I asked what the name meant, and Mr. Castleman said it was the Hebrew name for Esther.

He continued by saying, "In the Bible, the book of Esther tells the story of a Jewish woman married to the King of Persia who saved her people from extermination." Mr. Castleman suggested that one day I read it, for it had much to do with the path I was on. I let that comment slide. I still remember Hadassah, the parrot, to this day; her personality was like that of a human. If you talked to her, she responded as if she knew exactly what was being said.

After mentioning the book of Esther, Mr. Castleman said it was time to go deeper in our talks, and he blessed me with a beautiful leather Bible, stating, "This book will change your life." He explained, "The Bible is the infallible, incorruptible Word of God; it is truth that never changes.

"It consists of thirty-nine books in the Old Testament, which are about the time before Jesus Christ lived, and twenty-seven books in the New Testament, which are about Jesus's life and beyond. Some call the Bible the 'Word of God'; others call it 'a love letter to His children.'

"Without a doubt it is a guide that needs to be used daily by people for them to know how to live life to the fullest. It has practical applications for living today, even though it was written decades ago."

He continued by saying the Bible was inspired by the Spirit of God through man. I explained to Mr. Castleman that I had some Bibles in my bookshop, and I'd tried reading it once but had been unable to understand it.

Mr. Castleman said that was okay and understandable. The Bible contained secret truths and hidden messages only for those willing to know God and His Son. He encouraged me and said, "Together, we will learn, one step at a time." He also shared that as I spent time reading the Word of God, meditating in it, and writing it on the tablet of my heart, I would come to understand and see.

Mr. Castleman then gave me a brief overview of what the Bible was all about. I listened intently, and since he hadn't led me wrong yet, my gut was to trust him in this too.

My first assignment was to read Psalm 91 with Mr. Castleman. He showed me where the book of Psalms was in the Bible, and together we read,

> He who dwells in the secret place of the Most High
> Shall abide under the shadow of the Almighty.
> I will say of the LORD, "He is my refuge and my fortress;
> My God, in Him I will trust."
> Surely He shall deliver you from the snare of the fowler
> And from the perilous pestilence.
> He shall cover you with His feathers,
> And under His wings you shall take refuge;
> His truth shall be your shield and buckler.
> You shall not be afraid of the terror by night,
> Nor of the arrow that flies by day,
> Nor of the pestilence that walks in darkness,
> Nor of the destruction that lays waste at noonday.
> A thousand may fall at your side,
> And ten thousand at your right hand;
> But it shall not come near you.
> Only with your eyes shall you look,
> And see the reward of the wicked.
> Because you have made the LORD, who is my refuge,
> Even the Most High, your dwelling place,
> No evil shall befall you,
> Nor shall any plague come near your dwelling;
> For He shall give His angels charge over you,
> To keep you in all your ways.
> In their hands they shall bear you up,
> Lest you dash your foot against a stone.
> You shall tread upon the lion and the cobra,
> The young lion and the serpent you shall trample underfoot.
> Because he has set his love upon Me, therefore I will deliver him;
> I will set him on high, because he has known My name.

He shall call upon Me, and I will answer him;
I will be with him in trouble;
I will deliver him and honor him.
With long life I will satisfy him,
And show him My salvation.

My mind was whirling. I had never heard words with such depth, filled with so many hidden meanings. I was overwhelmed with all kinds of emotions. I felt fear seeping up deep within me. As usual, my initial reaction was to run, but something kept me there.

I shared with Mr. Castleman that I had immediately gotten stuck on the word *trust* as we read the psalm together. *Trust*, I thought. That was something lacking in my life. Given my history—our history, as natives—I knew only how to distrust; we were suspicious, cynical, angry—and rightly so. Mistrust was embedded deep in my people, and I had learned it well. I had trusted only two people throughout my life, and they were Mrs. Gregory, whom I still dearly missed, and now Mr. Castleman.

It would be quite a journey to move from this state of living to love and trust. I questioned silently, "How can I possibly trust this God I cannot see?" This question truly perplexed me.

CHAPTER 7

The Ultimate Gift of Love

At our next meeting, Mr. Castleman began by saying, "The ultimate gift in the world—that mankind has missed and completely misunderstood—is that God loves you! He is not selective, judgmental, or a respecter of person. It's not based on who you are, what your skin color or culture is, where you are in life, or what you have done. The Bible tells us that God is love. First John 4:8 says, 'He who does not love does not know God, for God is love.'

"Many will argue that they cannot love the way God loves, but if you really understand that you are created in His image, then you can love as God does," Mr. Castleman continued. "This is where we will begin today's lesson. Your native people from years past knew of Great Spirit, or Creator God, as some may have called Him. Many heard and were led by Great Spirit and even knew of a Savior to come. Some interpreted Creator God differently from the God of the Bible; others felt they were one and the same. That isn't the point, nor where we will focus. It is time you learn how much God loves you by learning about His Son, Jesus.

"At the beginning of time, God created Adam and Eve. They were deceived to believe they could be like God and chose to disobey and turn away from the One who had made them. Adam and Eve committed a great sin against God. As a result, all mankind lost their ability to commune with God. Because of this, we needed a man without sin to be our propitiation, a substitute to atone for man's evil choice and sinful nature. So God sent His Son, Jesus Christ, to save us."

Mr. Castleman continued, "Love never fails. It was the amazing grace and love of God that restored our broken relationship with Him through His Son. Jesus became man, born of the Virgin Mary, and walked on this earth for thirty-three and a half years. The last three years of His life were filled with miracles, healings, followers, and sadly, persecutions. God or Jesus Himself could have stopped what was to happen or called legions of angels to thwart the inevitable, but God's greater purpose needed to be accomplished for you and me. This was done through the humble devotion and love of Jesus. He was crucified and buried. Then on the third day, He rose from the dead, and He is now seated at the right hand of God, interceding on our behalf daily.

"More than two thousand years later, those who believe in Jesus Christ as the Son of God have a restored relationship with God the Father. Only those who come to know Jesus can know the Father God, the Creator of all things. This is called being 'born again' or 'saved.' It is not something well embraced even today. Many people believe numerous paths lead to God. Sadly, they are wrong." Mr. Castleman shared that one day he had clearly heard God in a small, quiet voice say to him, "Know you this, there is only one way, and it is through My Son."

Mr. Castleman explained that many different beliefs and religions taught people could obtain eternal salvation through actions by being good, but man would always fail. "That which man does through the flesh will reap only what the flesh can achieve," he said. "Jesus is the only path to eternal salvation. It is a relationship with the Father, the Son, and the Holy Spirit.

"Do not confuse this relationship with church rules, dogmas, and the ritualistic ways of the many Christian denominations. A true believer walks the way of Jesus. His first command, found in Luke 10:27, states, 'You shall love the Lord your God with all your heart, with all your soul, with all your strength, and with all your mind, and your neighbor as yourself.' This is Jesus's greatest command, which surpasses all others."

I listened intently, tears streaming down my face, as I struggled to comprehend what was being said. I knew deep inside I had just heard the truth, and it was resonating in my spirit. It was a day I will never forget.

Later that evening, in the stillness of my room, I wept uncontrollably. Not really understanding why I was so distraught, I cried out to God, asking Him to forgive me for all my past missteps and all my sins. It was then that I took a step of faith and proclaimed Jesus Christ as my Savior.

I fell to my knees, my head in my hands, bowing down. Suddenly, I felt this overwhelming presence of love around me. It was as though I were being cradled in the arms of Father God. Mr. Castleman had told me this feeling sometimes happens but not always. Everyone's experience is different, and there is no "right way" to experience God. It was *my* individual experience. He also told me that being saved isn't a feeling; it isn't based on emotions. It is a faith walk, a faith statement.

I remained in His presence as I drifted to sleep, exhausted from tears and past burdens, hoping to awaken to a new life—one now filled with love, hope, wonder, and—to my surprise—more lessons.

CHAPTER 8

The Day

Life with Mr. Castleman was challenging but always adventurous, tearful, fulfilling, healing, and joyful. He celebrated with me concerning my "new birth," and my lessons continued delving deeper and deeper into the Word of God. I couldn't imagine life without him.

I hiked up to the cabin, eager and ready for another lesson or fun adventure, as I often had. When I crossed the bridge, I called out, but today there was no answer. My heart began to sink. I slowly stepped onto the porch where we had sat just days before. I peeked through the window. My stomach turned, feeling as though the air had been knocked out of me. I couldn't breathe. Immediately I felt fear creep in, and panic rose through my being.

The first thing I saw was that Hadassah wasn't in her cage, and the walking stick Mr. Castleman used was gone. *Calm down*, I thought. *He must be out for a walk.* But in my spirit, I knew that wasn't the case. I tried the door, and to my surprise, it was open. I slowly stepped inside, and sitting on the table was a note from Mr. Castleman. With shaking hands, I picked it up.

> My work is done here. It is time to move on.
> You now have all you will ever need, the ultimate gift of love.
> Now go forth; walk the Jesus way, for you are called.
> Fondly farewell,
> Mr. Bob Castleman, A. D.

Over and over, I read the note, hoping for answers, anything, but there was nothing. Mr. Castleman was gone.

That's it, I thought as tears rolled down my cheek. *That's it? That's all I get? After spending all this time with him? He just leaves. He disappears without so much as a word.*

Swirling and reeling, I had to sit before I passed out. I was in shock. Indeed, I knew a day would come when he would no longer be here, but that didn't go as I expected. *How could he? How could he just leave and not even say goodbye?* Disbelief was all that kept going through my mind; the only man I had ever trusted, the very man who had helped me trust again, had disappeared.

The days swirled by. I was numb. I replayed our time together. As I thought back, I remembered Mr. Castleman telling me, "There has been a paradigm shift." I had no clue what that meant at the time and chose to simply ignore it.

I slowly found myself slipping back into the frame of mind I had been in before I met Mr. Castleman. I didn't pick up the Bible. I didn't pray. I was angry at God, at Mr. Castleman, and at anyone else who crossed my path.

Journeys was struggling, and I didn't care. I wallowed and whined even though I recalled Mr. Castleman telling me whining was what the Israelites had done while in the desert, and it had gotten them nowhere. I felt hopeless again; my focus was on me and my situation. I had no peace, joy, or vision for the future … again! I had no friends, many fears, and nothing to live for—or so I thought.

The Holy Spirit was continually urging me to go for a walk, but I fought that too. Early one morning, unable to sleep, I again picked up the note Mr. Castleman had left. This time when I read it, my eyes went right to "A. D." as if it were highlighted by the early-morning light. Why hadn't I seen that before?

My mind brought me back to the day I had found the business card Mr. Castleman left that said "B. C." I quickly pulled out my computer, looked up "A. D.," and learned it stood for anno Domini, Latin for "year of our Lord," indicating the number of years since the birth of Jesus Christ. It was the first time in weeks I'd felt some peace, and a slight smile crossed my face.

The Holy Spirit reminded me that Mr. Castleman was a gift from God; he had come to me "B. C.," before I knew Christ. I was to be grateful for the time we spent together and embrace all the lessons. This was my "year of the Lord," which meant it was time to walk the talk and be all God had created me to be for His glory and purpose. I wept and asked for forgiveness. I had forsaken God, but He never left me, as promised.

I went for a walk that day to the old, familiar places and found some new ones as well, being led step-by-step by the Holy Spirit. He showed me it was time for me to focus on Psalm 46:10: "Be still, and know that I AM God." That is what I did for days, weeks, and months until the peace of God fell on me. I then realized I couldn't depend on Mr. Castleman or others to fulfill me or make me happy. It was only through a deep relationship with Jesus Christ that the voids in life could be filled. Jesus truly is the ultimate gift of love to mankind; it is the love of God and a relationship with Him that would make my life complete.

One quiet summer afternoon, floating on the river in my kayak, I clearly heard from God what I was to do next with my life. Through the love of Mr. Castleman, the profound ultimate love of Creator God and Yeshua, I had found myself. It was time to walk the Jesus way in life and fulfill my purpose. It was time for me to return to my people and share the love I had found.

The Holy Spirit reminded me of Esther's story and that Mr. Castleman had said it had much to do with my path. Indeed, it was time to meditate deeper in the book of Esther. I now knew that Abba God, His Word, the Holy Spirit, and the love of Yeshua would assuredly show me the way. Faith steps were all I needed.

I praised God with drums, rattles, sticks, bells, and songs. I lifted my hands with thanksgiving. I danced as David had with my bells and worshipped the King of kings. I had found my purpose, my calling.

I shall always remember Mr. Castleman fondly and keep him in my prayers, sending love and strength his way—wherever he may be—knowing he is fulfilling his next calling in service to Abba. I have moved beyond anger to thankfulness, complete gratitude, and love for Mr. Castleman. I shall never forget him, all he taught and sacrificed for me. I do, however, look forward to the day when we meet again, either on earth or in the heavenly realm.

I'm now at peace. The Holy Spirit has called me back home to the reservation and has instructed me to teach all I have learned to my people. It is critical. I must share the good news of Creator God, Yahweh, and His Son, Yeshua, Jesus, the Christ. My people must know they are loved.

My name is Shawana, daughter of the Creator God, a disciple of Yeshua, and blessed to be a "keeper of my people," "Ganawenjige Anishinaabekaa," for the glory of God and His kingdom.

CHAPTER 9

Epilogue—Open Your Hearts

Everyone has a story. Life is a series of journeys bookended by past joy or pain and a future of hope or despair. My prayer is that you gleaned tidbits of hope and encouragement from Shawana's story.

I pray that you have received the same life-changing gift, the love of God and His Son, into your life. You are created in His image and are truly loved.

This journey called life isn't trouble free, but it is more bearable with the Creator of all things loving you. Jesus, the Christ (Yahshua, Yeshua, or Yahusha, as some call Him), sits at the right hand of God and is continually interceding on our behalf. All you need to do is ask and receive. What a blessing this is! What a gift of love!

In closing, Abba often gives me a word of encouragement, and here is one for you:

> Awaken, my child, awaken. Open your hearts to the love of My Son, and you will come to know Me as well. It is only through Him that we can commune. You only need to believe in Him, and you too will become

My son or my daughter eternally. I will be your Father forevermore.

Seek no other paths, for the truth lies here in this parable of love. Seek no other people, but dwell in My Word, and understanding will be yours.

I have prepared a purpose for each of My children, and only by drawing close will you find the way. Only through My Son will you see the way, the truth, and the life that I have ordained for you.

You are my unique creation, and I love you.
Be still and know Me.

Be of good cheer, for My Son has now set you free.

A PARABLE OF FORGIVENESS

Dear Children,

This parable of forgiveness takes you on a journey through the eyes of Shawana, a young First Nation woman. It is relevant to her beautiful people and all people who have suffered at the hand of another.

Unresolved forgiveness creates a life of anger, strife, and hatred. If one chooses to remain unforgiving, there can be no peace personally, corporately, or worldwide.

This parable is for anyone bitter, angry, hurt, lost, sick, and living with no hope. It is for any and all people who have had injustices done to them due to the mere fact that they exist and were "in the way." And it is for those who have been bullied, cast down by society, peers, family, or acquaintances.

May this parable lift your spirits and bring new hope to you. May you be renewed with a desire to live life to the fullest and accomplish what Creator God ordained for you. You are His unique creation, and you are loved.

God's blessings and peace ~

CHAPTER 1

Walking the Jesus Way

It took much longer than I expected to wrap things up at my small bookshop, Journeys, though I have to admit I wasn't in any hurry to return to the reservation, even knowing I had a calling on my life to do so.

Kayaking had become a treasured pastime for me, and I was concerned that I wouldn't have the opportunity there. I was also profoundly afraid that I would be drawn back into the world I had left, losing all I had learned over the past years. I knew deep in my spirit that I wasn't really trusting Abba with this type of thinking; it was just procrastination.

It is incredible how easily one can explain stalling. For me, I kept saying I needed to do this for my health. The closeness of the water always drew me in and brought peace to my body, soul, and spirit. Whether it was walking, kayaking, or sitting in God's creation, I found it was something I needed to do daily to remain grounded in Him.

God's creation was a wonder to me, like watching the herons standing at the water's edge, searching for fish or perching high in the trees. It always brought a smile to my face when they gawked at me as I paddled by. Likewise, the beavers fascinated me with their diligence and unwavering focus on building their dams, gathering food, and slapping their flat tails when I got too close. Early morning or late evening was always the best time to watch the beavers, and if fortunate, I watched the baby beavers swim and play.

Once I was blessed to see a family of common merganser ducks. They flew in and landed on the river in a perfectly straight line, ten of them. I chuckled each time their butts stuck up out of the water as they dove before coming up with small whitefish in their beaks. They weren't the most colorful ducks I had seen, certainly not like the mallards. Common mergansers have gray-colored heads and crowns, orange beaks, brown bodies, and all-white undersides. Regardless, I spent hours watching them.

The lessons I had gleaned from God's creation would sustain me in the most challenging days that were to come. Take, for instance, the duck. The oils on the duck's feathers allow water to stream over them, resulting in one of my favorite sayings, "Just let that stressful situation or criticism flow off your back like water on a duck."

Sitting amid God's creation always brought to remembrance my dear friend Mr. Castleman. He had a special connection with nature and animals that was greater than most humans. He told me about an owl that had been injured as a fledgling and that he'd nurtured it back to health. The bond created between the two lasted a lifetime. I will never forget the day I heard the owl calling out. It was early evening, and we were on one of our many hikes. Suddenly, Mr. Castleman called back, and this vast owl came soaring down and landed on his extended arm. It was massive yet beautiful. Within minutes it flew away. I was amazed, and Mr. Castleman explained it was like the bond we have with God; it would always be there.

That bond he talked about was similar to the one I had with him. It was a divine connection. It amused me how often he retold the story of how the leading of the Lord had sent him to my shop. He had been sitting in his cabin, enjoying quiet time, and reading the Bible when he clearly heard the Lord say, "Go meet the owner of the small bookshop in town." The day he stepped into my life was the day my life changed.

I had been at a point of desperation and hopelessness. I had no one. I had alienated myself from my family, I had no friends, and my future was bleak. I had inherited a small bookshop in the town of Graceville, New Hampshire. For a few years life was good. Mrs. Gregory, the owner, had become my family when she took me in without question. I had traveled far from home, desperate to get out and insistent I'd never go back. I grew up on a small rural reservation in northern North Dakota, home to the

Ojibway people. I had never felt like I belonged there during my entire childhood, and now I didn't belong in Graceville either.

Mr. Castleman thought otherwise, though. He became my mentor, a teacher of life. The minute he stepped into the shop, I saw unconditional love and light in his eyes. I thought, *That is something I want and need.* Mr. Castleman diligently taught me for almost three years before he was called to another assignment. Daily he would call or stop in to see me. It was as if he knew exactly where I was emotionally, spiritually, and physically. This knowledge frightened me initially; however, I learned it was really God, my Father, watching over me through His faithful servant.

Mr. Castleman gently and lovingly taught me some of my native heritage and showed me that God loves all His people, no matter color, race, or creed. This was evident by His Son and the work of the cross. Mr. Castleman talked to me without judgment, unlike others who supposedly shared the "good news." It was his Christlike love, the kind of love that accepted me for who I was, that led me to want to know who Jesus Christ was. I will never forget the day when Jesus or Yeshua, which I like to call Him, became my Savior, my life, my all in all.

After that life-changing moment and all the teachings Mr. Castleman gave me, there was a paradigm shift. I didn't recognize it immediately, but I finally found myself confident and able to stand independently. The change? I had Jesus. I found the love of my Father, and I had the Word of God to live by. Knowing all this didn't stop me from being devastated the day Mr. Castleman disappeared. I reeled from that shock for months but knew deep in my heart that I now had a calling and purpose, and that I no longer needed Mr. Castleman.

Before he left, he had told me I was to spend time in the book of Esther. Knowing that everything he did had a distinct purpose and intention, I did exactly as he suggested. The lessons I gleaned from Esther ignited deep within me the desire to help my people; they taught me how to step out in faith, even through fears, as Esther had. God had provided a means for her to save her people, and I, too, felt that calling as "keeper of my people." It was now time to head back home to the reservation and share what it meant to walk through life the Jesus way.

CHAPTER 2

Remembering My Past

Mr. Castleman taught me that without acknowledgment of sin, there cannot be forgiveness; without forgiveness, there is no reconciliation; and without reconciliation, there is no peace. This was the life I had been born into on the reservation some years before—a life with no peace or hope.

There was no one to blame, yet everyone was to blame. Through my healing journey, I learned I had to stop hiding my head in the sand by intentionally ignoring the past. It was time to embrace my culture; it was time to research my native history and uncover the truth instead of blindly believing what had been taught to me by ill-equipped schools—if they could even be called that given the scarcity of books and teachers on the Rez. Elders knew the truth. They tried to teach younger generations, but their bitterness and anger were concealed by drinking and drugs to numb the pain, forget the past, and not think about the future.

Now, after my time with Mr. Castleman, I was finally ready to embrace the true history and suffering my people endured. This was the moment I began my journey to forgiveness. I finally understood it wasn't the fault of my parents, whom I had continuously blamed as a child. It hadn't started with them, nor was it the result of what I saw happening daily on the Rez. I realized they were all suffering too.

The problem had started generations back. The defeated attitude and lack of belonging had begun when my native race was considered "less" than any other man or people group. We were deemed inferior or, as some would say, as "savages." This treatment began long ago when Columbus discovered our country, and we were captured, enslaved, and killed—all in pursuit of money, gold, spices, and the riches found in our land. Then, when we were in the way, we were removed.

Native Americans, First Nations people, had great respect for God's creation. We shared properties, lived in villages, and did everything together. Women took care of the crops and the children; men hunted for food. We were taught to respect our elders, and honor was given to the Creator. This was in great contrast to the European values of greed, self-gratification, and self-preservation. Columbus didn't enter a land of savages and wilderness; he entered a land of people who honored the Creator God, cared for each other, and worked as a community.

As Columbus traveled around the Caribbean, capturing First Nations people, known as the Arawaks, word spread throughout the villages. Soon my people began to fight back as women and children were being taken as slaves for sex and labor. If the white man couldn't find gold, then my people were punished, hunted down, and killed at their hands.

Columbus falsely believed that what he was doing was righteous and God driven. He used pious religious talk to seemingly mask and justify the complete annihilation of my people. After Columbus and the Spaniards' arrival, the population of Native Arawaks went from two hundred and fifty thousand to around only five hundred in just fifty years.

I was visibly distraught and openly wept, reading the gut-wrenching statistics I had found. As I continued, I told myself this research must be done so people could recognize the injustices we, First Nations people, continued to suffer. We all must move forward to overcome the abuse and embrace forgiveness.

Throughout history, European Americans have condemned cultural groups for not integrating into the American lifestyle; however, the rationalizations used to justify what was done to the First Nations people, a peaceful people, were atrocious. Bounties were put on my people's heads, varying from $25 to $130 for a male scalp, and it was usually half that amount for a woman's or child's. It was said, "The only good Indian was a dead one." As I read this, I realized this attitude had been accepted and even encouraged for more than four hundred years.

As I dug deeper into history, the abuse and destruction of my native people and their culture continued. To recount all the injustices would be impossible; however, I feel it is necessary to cover a couple of them for the healing process.

First, let me discuss the Trail of Tears. The Cherokee Nation was given two years to leave the land they occupied. When many wanted to stay in their homeland, seven thousand troops were sent to forcibly remove the people in 1830. They were made to march hundreds of miles to what is now Oklahoma. They were forced at bayonet point and held in stockades. About four thousand died from hunger, disease, and the trek through the treacherous, cold territory. The US government sanctioned this atrocity because someone wanted the land.

Recently, I saw an article about students hanging a banner for a sports function that said, "Hey, Indians, how about a trail of tears, round 2?" The school officials handled it well; however, the incident highlighted people's ignorance and the crucial need for resolutions across the nation. Clearly, healing hasn't begun; people are insensitive and unaware of the truth. Compassion is desperately lacking.

And then there is the massacre at Wounded Knee. Around 1888, the remaining Sioux were forced to go to reservations at gunpoint. An awakening began in the North American tribes, which were physically, emotionally, and spiritually broken. A holy man received a message from the Creator that they would soon be free from the white man. Hope grew, excitement spread, and some became defiant of the holy man's nonviolence belief. A ritual called the Ghost Dance spread through the north. Fearing a rebellion, South Dakota's settlers commanded that the ritual dance be discontinued. When this was ignored, the US Army interceded.

As tempers and fears escalated, about three hundred Sioux left the reservation and hesitantly agreed to be moved to Wounded Knee Creek or the Pine Ridge Reservation. On December 29, 1890, a gun was mistakenly fired when the army commanded surrendering Sioux weapons, and the Seventh Cavalry aggressively fired on the Sioux. Chief Big Foot was shot in his tent; others were killed as they tried to run away. Almost all three hundred men, women, and children were shot dead. Others died frozen in the snow.

This was about four hundred years after Columbus had come to this "uninhabited" land. The massacre at Wounded Knee was the last confrontation between First Nations people and the US Army. In 1890, the US census affirmed the frontier was now officially closed.

The government felt their proposal to permanently remove my people to government-run reservations was for their protection. The goal was to civilize my people until they were assimilated into the white man's culture.

We were encouraged to integrate and adapt to American culture. The intent was to improve tribal life. However, it did more destruction than good, which continues today throughout the nation. Alaskan villages have the highest suicide rate per capita in the United States, a suicide rate of almost four times the national average. The more youth are exposed to suicidal behavior, the more likely they become "just another statistic" to the rest of the world.

Extremely high suicide rates also exist on my reservation and many other tribal reservations in South Dakota, Montana, and Arizona (to name a few). Suicides are rampant among young children and teens, but parents, aunts, and uncles often also succumb to suicide to escape from the deplorable conditions.

Many First Nations people live in extreme poverty with little or no electricity and no running water; those lucky enough to have running water find it's often contaminated. A documentary released recently exposed the harsh living conditions of the Blackfeet, whose land became desolate as a result of drilling oil. The government was cheating the landholders out of millions of dollars, and Elouise Cobbell filed a lawsuit against the United States for proper retribution.[5] These inhumane conditions and injustices need to be recognized and addressed before healing and forgiveness can be achieved. The first step is acknowledgment.

Forced assimilation of the First Nations people effectively destroyed us: body, soul, and spirit. But after that, what is left? History proves we have become a people without self-value, without a home, without a country; and this hopelessness continues today.

---

[5] *100 Years; One Woman's Fight for Justice*, directed by Melinda Janko, (Fire in the Belly Productions, Inc., 2016), https://www.100yearsthemovie.com/

CHAPTER 3

Journey to My People

The day finally came when I closed up Journeys, and my belongings were packed. Before leaving Graceville, I took one last walk up to Mr. Castleman's cabin, secretly hoping he had come back and I would find him there one last time before my departure. I was again disappointed and saddened when I saw no signs of life. The cabin was still in good shape, considering it had been abandoned for a season or two, and I was surprised to find the peace I had always felt there was still present, even in his absence.

I walked to a few of my favorite spots for one last look. As usual, I was blessed by a stroll through God's creation. The benches at the pond were welcoming. I sat for a while on the seat situated in the sun. I soaked up the warmth because I was chilled after walking through the cool, shady woods. The heat from the sun warmed not only my physical body but also my spiritual being. As I bathed in this moment, the presence of the Lord came upon me, and I heard the Lord clearly say to me,

> My daughter, the time is now. You have significant work to be done, and I am calling you. For far too long, unforgiveness has blocked blessings on My people. One cannot walk in love and hold bitterness in his or her heart.

The greatest command given to mankind is to love one another as I have loved you. This cannot happen if there is strife and unforgiveness throughout the land.

You have learned much. You are ready, and I will be with you each step of the way. The journey may not be comfortable, but it is critical.

A great awakening has started, and for that to continue, there must be forgiveness. My Son at the cross prepared the way, but mankind has gotten distracted from His finished work, from My love, from My way.

Go forth, My daughter. Fulfill that which I ordained from the beginning of time. Be still and listen for guidance. Go forth in peace.

My heart pounded in my chest. I knew it was the voice of God, and I must be about my Father's business. I headed back to the shop, picked up my bag, and made the next bus connection to North Dakota. The route was more than a day long with at least four stops, so I settled in for my journey home. I took this time to meditate in the Word, listen for instructions from the Holy Spirit, rest, pray, and bathe in His presence. It had been many years since I was back home, and not being sure of what kind of reception I would get, I was a bit apprehensive. Casting my care on Him, though, I was reassured by reading Isaiah 61:1–3.

> The Spirit of the Lord GOD is upon Me,
> Because the LORD has anointed Me
> To preach good tidings to the poor;
> He has sent Me to heal the brokenhearted,
> To proclaim liberty to the captives,
> And the opening of the prison to those who are bound;
> To proclaim the acceptable year of the LORD,
> And the day of vengeance of our God;
> To comfort all who mourn,
> To console those who mourn in Zion,

> To give them beauty for ashes,
> The oil of joy for mourning,
> The garment of praise for the spirit of heaviness;
> That they may be called trees of righteousness,
> The planting of the LORD, that He may be glorified.

The trip went faster than I'd expected, and soon I would be stepping back in time to a time I would just as soon have forgotten if it wasn't for my calling from Creator God. To prepare, I recalled what I had researched in current articles in print and on the Internet before leaving.

My home was one of the largest First Nations communities; the reservation had a population of twenty-three hundred to three thousand living on just under forty-five hundred acres. The Ojibway people value their way of life, language, family, and traditions.

What had once been a thriving community that flourished by hunting, trapping, fishing, gathering, and living on the land was now a community in crisis. Statistics reported that an estimated 75 percent of the population was under twenty-five, and unemployment was over 90 percent. The entire population lived in about 375 homes. Due to the lack of housing, families needed to sleep in shifts. A diesel generator provided power to the community, and 80 percent of the homes didn't have clean running water or sewage systems.

I'd heard that the reservation's only school had burned to the ground in 2007, but I was encouraged when I read a new one had been built in 2016. Life was hard on the Rez. There was no work, inadequate education, no health care or security, and there had been a boil water advisory for over ten years due to the lack of power from the generator. Alcoholism, domestic abuse, depression, drug use, solvent abuse, and sniffing gas had become a way of life for many. Often women were abused or simply disappeared. I had fled to New Hampshire as the suicide rate hit an all-time high, knowing I could be next.

I had read that the community would soon have a counselor for every one hundred residents, which was great, but the root cause still needed to be addressed. I also learned that the federal government had provided $27 million to connect our reservation to the power grid. I wondered how long that would take to happen, instinctively skeptical—an inherited trait among us natives, something we learned from generations before us.

I lived in a remote rural community accessible only by airplane and a few unkempt roads. All the counseling in the world couldn't help; more than anything, they were in desperate need of employment to provide for their families. Our community grew fast when federal subsidies were provided, but with subsidies came the deterioration of living conditions and violent crime.

The federal government believed what they were doing was helpful for tribes across the United States. They said they intended to help; however, I think the root cause of my people's demise was what had happened to my relatives not too far back in history.

Our land was taken from us, and we were moved to reservations. Christian missionaries came in and urged or forced my people to abandon their old traditions. Elders who had experienced this pressure firsthand talked openly about the boarding schools the Christian missionaries ran. They described that ministers took native children from their families and put them in the schools. They cut the children's hair, changed their clothes, and beat them if they spoke their native language. The missionaries did everything they could to assimilate us into the "white man's world." We were crushed; our spirits were broken, and our souls were destroyed. We belonged nowhere, had no dignity, and our self-worth was annihilated.

I remembered reading a statement by Clyde Warrior, a Ponca, president of the National Indian Youth Council in 1967. He captured the life of my people with his words:

> *Most [of us] ... can remember when we were children and spent many hours at the feet of our grandfathers listening to stories of the time when the Indians were a great people, when we were free, when we were rich, when we lived the good life.*
>
> *At the same time we heard stories of droughts, famines and pestilence. It was only recently that we realized that there was surely great material deprivation in those days, but that our old people felt rich because they were free.*
>
> *They were rich in the things of the spirit, but if there is one that characterizes Indian life today it is poverty of the spirit.*

We still have human passions and depth of feeling, (which may be something rare these days), but we are poor in spirit because we are not free—free in the most basic sense of the word.

We are not allowed to make those basic human choices and decisions about our personal life and about the destiny of our communities which is the mark of free mature people. We sit on our front porches or in our yards, and the world and our lives in it pass us by without our desires or aspirations having any effect.

We are not free. We do not make choices. Our choices are made for us; we are the poor ... We have many rulers ... They call us into meetings and tell us what is good for us and how they've programmed us, or they come into our homes to instruct us and their manners are not always what one would call polite by Indian standards or perhaps any standards.

We are rarely accorded respect as fellow human beings. Our children come home from school to us with shame in their hearts and a sneer on their lips for their home and parents.

We are the "poverty problem" and that is true; and perhaps it is also true that our lack of reasonable choices, our lack of freedom, our poverty spirit is not unconnected with our material poverty.[6]

---

[6] James Wilson, *The Earth Shall Weep, A History of Native America*, (New York, NY: Grove Press, 1999), 370–371.

CHAPTER 4

Reconnecting

Indeed, I never would have expected to be hugged so tightly that I could hardly breathe as tears fell freely from my family member's eyes. I wept as I hugged each one of them, so happy to see them yet ashamed and full of remorse for the way I'd left.

It was a moment I will never forget, for I was embraced as the prodigal son in Luke 15:20. "And he arose and came to his father. But when he was still a great way off, his father saw him and had compassion, and ran and fell on his neck and kissed him." Abba is good and faithful.

We spent quite a bit of time catching up and sharing a meal of my favorites: "fry bread" and "Three Sisters Soup" (corn, beans, and squash). I was amazed at how comfortable I felt there and reveled in the fact that all the anger and anxiety I had once held was now gone. I quietly thanked Yeshua for His peace that surpassed all my understanding.

I was ever so grateful that there was a room for me to share with one of my sisters. She had been a young girl when I left, so I hoped we could catch up and get to know each other again. This wasn't an easy process, but the Creator managed to break down the walls between us.

I didn't yet bring up my salvation and that I now walked the Jesus way. From my experience, I knew it was crucial not to push. Abba showed me just to let my love and light shine, and as time went on, He and the Holy Spirit would create the perfect opportunities to share.

My dad was still primarily unemployed, and I could see the pain in his eyes. The inability to provide for one's family shatters self-esteem; it indeed has brought many men from all walks of life into a deep depression. I was thankful that my dad hadn't given up and daily looked for work. Occasionally he found it. My mom was still the keeper of the home and did a fantastic job, considering the absence of necessities like clean water and heat. She also had to deal with a roof that leaked. I realized my family had a determination some of my Ojibway brothers and sisters lacked. I was grateful for that. It was something I hadn't seen before I left.

One afternoon, I talked to my youngest sister, Aki, and heard what life had been like on the Rez from her perspective. With tears in her eyes, she shared that a school friend, only fifteen years old, had just committed suicide. Aki continued to say that this friend had left behind parents who had recently lost another son and nephew to suicide and that four more teens had committed suicide earlier that month. Usually her classmates handled this stress by huffing gas, getting drunk, or recklessly driving at high speeds to get away and shut down the pain, but they had made a different choice this time.

A group of thirty teens chose to help the families who had lost children instead of diving into the darkness of grief and despair. They had cooked meals, ran errands, cleaned, cut grass, fixed broken items, and gathered clean water in jugs for the families. Aki said it had been such an amazing sight. The focus was to be selfless instead of selfish, and the service lifted their spirits more than huffing gas ever could.

I was pleased to see this positive movement in the youth, but without Yeshua, they had a long way to go. The Holy Spirit reminded me it wasn't time to share about Jesus and directed me to visit the elders.

This time I saw my elders with different eyes, with the eyes of Jesus. Judgments had fallen by the wayside, and a spirit of love and compassion filled my being. My heart broke as I listened to them share stories of their past with fresh ears and a new respect. After the government and Christian missionaries had invaded our land to "rescue" my people, the atrocities and alienations continued—even to this day.

I listened as my uncle told the story of how he had learned long ago from his elders about a Savior who would come and walk among the people. "When the missionaries came," he said, "many were excited, hoping this might be the Savior we heard about long ago. However, as the different missionaries came and shared about Jesus, they each came with different interpretations of the Bible and denominations. Our people became confused as the different missionaries told them, 'No, the Baptists are wrong. The only path to Savior is the Methodist denomination.' It was the same for Roman Catholics and any others who came to rescue us."

I couldn't even imagine how that must have been. My people weren't taught about the love of a Savior or of a loving Father as I had been. My uncle continued, telling me that he had decided to check out a little white Lutheran church one day not too far from where he lived. As he entered, he was greeted with looks and whispers, for his clothes and hair were different from the rest. He sat in the back, knowing that would be the only place he could sit inconspicuously, but even that measure didn't work.

He felt ashamed and unloved. After the service, the pastor talked to him about "fitting in better" by dressing "more appropriately." From that day on, my uncle never set foot in a church again. He went home and tried to rub his skin color off, desiring to fit in and be loved. He was searching for and wanting to learn about a Savior but found only rejection.

One may think this story happened generations ago, but that's not the case. I felt the same when I was in Graceville. Most looked at me strangely and had the stereotypical preconception that I was a "lazy, no good Indian." However, I was blessed by the people God brought into my life who weren't of that manner.

It deeply saddened me that my people still weren't accepted and felt hopeless, ashamed, and abused. I understood their anger, but I had finally found the key to overcoming it and knew there was hope. I intimately knew a Savior who had come to save the lost and unloved, and soon I would openly share this news with my people.

CHAPTER 5

Building Bridges of Trust

I deeply and personally understand what it means to experience hopelessness, abuse, anger, and despair. I grew up with it. I know the lack of trust buried within a soul. These shackles run deep through generations of people. The bonds appear in life as guilt, shame, skepticism, rejection, loneliness, insecurity, and feelings of worthlessness. A life filled with these burdens is a life without hope leading to depression, addiction, heartbreak, and sadly, death.

My people's past has been embedded in their souls, for they lived with these bondages daily—and it broke my heart. However, as I had come to find, Jesus could and would free them from these shackles. Mr. Castleman taught me that reconciliation was an instrumental part of healing and restoration, not meant for my people alone but for any cultural group or individual that has been treated inhumanely.

I learned that by walking the Jesus way and with the Word, one could learn to heal from past injustices and deep, soulful wounds and move toward building bridges of forgiveness. One evening in my prayer time, the Holy Spirit started to give me instructions on how this healing process was to begin. He instructed me that the walls must be broken down with love and compassion and that I must take this journey with them.

Self-work isn't easy. Looking into our souls exposes things we aren't proud of at times, and it's easier just to walk away. The wall of shame and insecurity must be broken so others can realize Jesus unconditionally loves them just the way they are. Thankfully, the Holy Spirit directs each step.

I began holding casual meetings in the community hall. At first, not many people came, but the room was filled with all ages after a while. I told stories of my trip to New Hampshire, my bookshop, and all the people I had met. My audience was intrigued and wanted to learn more about life off the Rez. I carefully listened to the Holy Spirit, only speaking what I was directed to share, realizing too much too soon could frighten some. I was compassionate, loving, and respectful of those with a deeply embedded fear rooted in distrust. I knew from personal experience that change isn't easy or well received.

As Mr. Castleman had taught me, building trust was the first step to open communication, so I stepped cautiously each time we met, striving again to earn the trust of my people. I shared the lessons I had learned about the north, south, east, and west—and about the instruments that reflected those directions. This topic seemed to pique their interest, especially the drums.

The Holy Spirit quietly spoke to my spirit and said, "This will be a way to communicate and build trust. Go throughout the community and borrow handheld drums, bells, sticks, and rattles." I was amazed at how much excitement this activity created. It even caught some of the teens' attentions. By the next meeting, there were many new faces. I quietly thanked Abba.

That evening I began with a talk about oneness, which my people truly understood, for throughout generations, they had walked closely with the Creator. They understood the need to honor creation and to be one with it, since mankind relied on it to live. Listening to the Holy Spirit's prompting, I shared about Father God; His Son, Jesus; and the Holy Spirit. Though they are separate, they are one. Most people understandably found this teaching extremely difficult to comprehend. I used my people's harmony with Creator, creation, and each other, and they were able to better understand the concept that evening.

As I learned from Mr. Castleman, teaching by participation has a lasting effect, so I continued by explaining what we were about to do. I shared that when a group of people gathered together to play instruments, first, it would be chaotic with no continuous beat. However, as all of them listened with their hearts, a natural rhythm would evolve, and they would all beat as one. I then stated, "This is what it is like to be close to Savior Jesus, to be one with Him. It's like we become one heartbeat with Jesus."

As the instruments were passed out, the hesitations and insecurities were obvious. When we began, the fear and lack of trust in many eyes saddened me, but Holy Spirit was faithful. As I watched, I witnessed the chaotic beats slowly evolve into a single, rhythmic beat resounding through the building. I saw walls start to break down. I noticed flickers of joy breaking through my people's beautiful faces.

Bridges of trust began developing, and slowly many started to see and feel the lesson of oneness. It was an exuberant time as we explored the beat of the drum. I encouraged each person to take a turn starting a drumbeat, and all were amazed at how each time we would progress into one steady beat.

My people learned they were each essential to the whole. A beat without them wasn't the same—there was a part, something, missing. I added, "This is the way the Creator sees His children." I watched as the shyness, hesitation, and insecurity dissipated as the night went on. It was a great lesson in unity, one mind with Christ, and that a gathering of two or more can move a mountain. I began to see glimmers of hope. Later that evening, I wept with joy, for God was genuinely moving among my tribe.

In the following weeks, my lessons continued. One evening I gathered the teens and told them we were going to make face masks. I suggested they think about how they felt others perceived them but urged them to make their masks reflections of who they were on the inside. A quiet excitement swept through the group as they whispered to each other. Secretly again, I thanked Abba.

At the next meeting, we began the face mask meeting by pairing off. Realizing this would be a great lesson in trust and dependency, I watched as the participants cautiously selected a partner. These teens had experienced so much; trust wasn't freely given, even among each other. With loving encouragement, they eventually paired off.

We began as partners, carefully putting Vaseline on each other's faces, mindful to keep the eyes and mouth free. They had the option of doing a whole mask or half. I then placed strips of papier mâché over the beautiful young faces, and everyone lay still on mats as the masks dried.

I unobtrusively put some native flute music on my CD player to calm any residual restlessness as everyone remained still for an hour as the paper strips hardened. In the stillness of the room, I spoke about the love of Abba and His Son. I told them about how much the Creator loved them and that they weren't—nor would they ever be—forgotten. As the masks dried, the peace of Jesus came upon the room. I knew without a doubt that the Holy Spirit had led me through this workshop; His presence brought the spirit of reconciliation to these young people.

The excitement began to build in the room as we started to remove the set masks. What a joy to see! We broke for lunch as the masks dried further, and then I brought out paint, feathers, jewels, beads, and glitter. I was amazed as the teens finished masterpieces depicting who they thought they were. The masks truly reflected the resilience of these strong individuals. Some of the most beautiful masks reflected the inner struggles of shame and anger. I was well pleased, for this indeed indicated that the healing process had begun.

At the next community meeting, we set the masks on display for all to see. Each participant came to the front to describe his or her creation. Each teen proudly presented his or her mask to the elders and parents. It was clear the teens had been empowered through this process and finally grateful for being accepted for who they were—some for the first time ever. The healing continued.

In the following gatherings, I talked about recognizing and acknowledging the injustices done to First Nations peoples throughout generations, including the horrors suffered at the hands of Christian missionaries. I shared that without recognition, there could be no forgiveness. Some felt they had no reason to forgive—what had happened to them had just been wrong. I understood that and acknowledged their feelings.

I shared that we needed to forgive and overcome—not only for our personal benefit and health but also for the sake of our First Nations. Living in anger and hate wasn't the Creator's way. In addition, I explained that we would need to gather with non-native people in the future so they could seek forgiveness, repent, and make amends for the injustices done.

Only then would the country be healed. This is God's way of walking in love and forgiveness for the sake of all involved.

Soon the day came when the Holy Spirit said, "Now is the time. Tell them about Savior Jesus this evening." By His grace, earlier that day, I had found a native translation of Hebrews 1:1–3. This was perfection, so I shared the elder's interpretation of this scripture.

> Long ago Creator spoke many times and in many ways to our ancestors through prophets. But now in these final days, He has spoken to us through His Son. Creator promised everything to the Son as an inheritance, and through the Son He made the universe and everything in it. The Son reflects the Creator's own glory, and everything about him represents Creator exactly. He sustains the universe by the mighty power of his command. I like this last one because it connects us to our ancestors. All the promises He made to them are fulfilled in Jesus. He is the One who created the world.
>
> He created the water where we go pray in the mornings. He created the fire where we dance and sing. He created the turtles where we get our rattles. He created the smoke that raises up to honor Him. To me it says that any ceremony that is from the Great Spirit will point to Him. If it is true, then it will point to the Truth. Everything that is true will point to Him. He is the fulfillment of the sacred fire, the cleansing fire, the water ceremonies, the sweat lodge and all other things. They all point to Him …
>
> When I pray at water I know He is the One I am thanking. When I dance, I dance to Him. When I bless myself with cedar fire, I am realizing that it is His Blood that cleanses me. And when I sweat in the O'si, I am thanking Him for a cleansing that never ends.[7]

---

[7] Corky Alexander, *Native American Pentecost, Praxis, Contextualization, Transformation*, (Tennessee: Cherohala Press, 2012), 149-150.

A hush had fallen over the room. I continued by saying, "This is the true Son of God, Jesus the Christ, Yeshua, the one who will save and guide us through all things in life. This is the same Savior our elders heard of from missionaries; however, many of these ministers sadly missed the Savior's pure heart of unconditional love and acceptance.

"A great heartbreak occurred in us when the truth was corrupted by man's ego. Man's biblical interpretations became religious, legalistic rules and dogmas that became more important than following God's Word. Missionaries didn't accept us unconditionally. They did not teach that walking the Jesus path in life, honoring God Creator, and living with the Holy Spirit's guidance is the only way to a peaceful life.

"There is healing through Jesus. You can overcome, for there is forgiveness and reconciliation through Jesus. He is the way, the truth, and the life." I then shared my story of when I had accepted Yeshua into my life and called those forward who also wanted this free gift. The Holy Spirit moved mightily. The front of the room was filled as my brothers and sisters came forward, and I led them in a prayer to accept Yeshua as their Savior. We hugged and wept. The love enveloping the room that evening was undeniable, and for many of my people, it was the first time they had felt loved.

CHAPTER 6

The Ultimate Gift of Forgiveness

Among First Nations people, when one mentions forgiveness, defenses immediately arise. "Why should I forgive? What good would it do me? I am owed an apology or restitution. It's not my fault." And the comments can go on and on.

History has shown us that my people experienced horrific demoralization at the hand of those who attempted to destroy our culture. What other people throughout history have had to endure such atrocities? Immediately one thinks of the Jewish people, the Holocaust, and Hitler. The difference therein is that the world recognized this injustice and supported the oppressed people group, a war was fought, and the people were set free.

This wasn't the case with First Nations people; no one came to our aid. Even today, more than five hundred years later, we still essentially stand alone. We were a people who existed peacefully on the land before the "white man" arrived. We haven't been provided proper restitution, nor has our land been restored. Apologies haven't been offered. Why were my people stripped of their identity, forced to reservations, and subjected to inhumane living conditions? For the sake of the government, the wealth of others, and the expansion of Christianity?

Anger runs deep. As I was researching in preparation for my trip home, I found "Thanksgiving Poem" by Jonathan Garfield. A few lines say it all:

> Thank you for relocating relations, relocating their hearts, some forgetting or ashamed of their Indigenous roots.
>
> Thank you for Catholic boarding school surgeons painfully removing our Native tongue without anesthetic until our mouths bled English.
>
> Thank you for the children starving reservations wide, left alone and staying up late, hoping their parent or parents didn't drink or shoot up all the check.
>
> Thank you for the Reservation suicides that have killed the spirits of those left behind.[8]

Unforgiveness keeps us in bondage; it tortures our souls and leads to anger in every area of life. Unforgiveness is controlling and destructive, and it creates divisions. It separates families and incites violence and war, hate crimes, addiction, cancer, disease, depression, and much more. It prevents us from living the life God intended for His children and blocks blessings.

I was once consumed with a fierce spirit of unforgiveness and anger and would say, "My anger is justified." I refused to soften my heart or stray from this state. I had to look deep within and ask, Is this truly the way to live? Do I want to be consumed with hate, pain, strife, and unforgiveness? Living this way was indeed not walking the Jesus way in life. Even on the cross, Jesus prayed, "Father, forgive them, for they do not know they do" (Luke 23:34).

As a believer, I needed to make a drastic change. This became one of the hardest lessons yet. I realized that if Jesus could forgive those who had crucified Him, I too can and must forgive the past injustices done to my

---

[8] Jonathan Garfield, *A Thanksgiving Poem by Jonathan Garfield*, Indian Country Today Media Network, https://newsmaven.io/indiancountrytoday/archive/thanksgiving-a-poem-by-jonathan-garfield-hHK2ksuqskKKLO8spK8SSw/, November 28, 2013.

people and me. This was the second ultimate gift from the Savior, which changed my life—forgiveness.

Mr. Castleman taught that strife isn't the walk of a follower of Jesus. He said, "Discontentment is a dangerous place to live." He asked, "Do you really want to poison your life daily with unforgiveness, angry thoughts, and words?" He then shared that God wants us to pray for our enemies. Matthew 5:44 says, "But I say unto you, love your enemies, bless those who curse you, do good to those who hate you, and pray for those who spitefully use you and persecute you."

Hastily I replied, "This is so unfair. They don't deserve my prayers."

Mr. Castleman chuckled and calmly responded, "That is not the point. God says pray for them. Forgiveness is for your sake, not for the sake of the offender. In forgiveness, you will elevate yourself to a place of blessing and favor in the Creator's eyes." He then continued teaching by stating, "That is being a believer in the Savior. We are not to walk by the flesh or feelings; this new way of living is to be a life of faith."

It wasn't easy. In fact, it was a gut-wrenching challenge at times. But God said to pray, so I did. God said to bless my enemies, not to curse them or speak evil, so slowly I did. Over time this brought me to new levels of love and compassion. When my flesh was winning and I still felt anger over the injustices, I cried out to Abba, and He helped me with my hardened heart. Eventually, Jesus provided the way for me to overcome and begin to release my anger and heal my soul.

My thinking was gradually changing; my mind was being renewed by Mr. Castleman's teachings. With daily time spent reading and meditating in the Word, I slowly transformed from a carnal/flesh-driven life to a Spirit-led life, which in turn began to heal my soul and help me move past any unresolved anger issues. I am so grateful to the Savior and this healing path; however, I remained perplexed about how to relay this ultimate gift of forgiveness to my people. I prayed and quietly asked the Holy Spirit for guidance.

CHAPTER 7

A Stranger in Town

Mr. Castleman's teachings, I realize now, were always taught in God's divine time. All that he imparted to me prepared me to teach my brothers and sisters. I shared that man is made of body, soul, and spirit—that we are triune beings just like God. Creator God functions as a Father, a Son, and the Holy Spirit, our great Comforter. We are a reflection of Him.

Mr. Castleman said the Bible, also known as the Word, would set me free. He said it contains "dunamis power"—a miracle-performing power—that can change lives. It serves as a guide on how we should live daily. It can heal the body, emotions, and spirit if we spend time absorbing the Word until it becomes more real internally than what we observe in the natural world.

I was taught that either we are walking in the God kind of love, or we are walking in fear. The Word teaches that perfect love casts out all fear. In love, there is no fear; therefore, when fear rose in my life, I was to monitor my thoughts, taking note of where my focus was. All fears and worries must be captured and replaced by the Word, which is truth.

All these lessons were remarkable and life changing, but truthfully, it wasn't a comfortable journey. I remember being so distraught, crying at the river and lying on the cool, damp ground, when I heard the Lord say to me, "You have a choice: stay here and wallow in your past or get up, release the pain, and move on." The Holy Spirit quietly whispered, "This is where you begin with your people. Help them release their pain. Let the Savior be the example."

Our weekly gatherings continued, and I saw a community of believers coming together step by step. By the leading of the Lord, I began Sunday worship gatherings. We sang and danced unto the Lord in our regalia, with our instruments and dark-colored skin. We were loved and accepted unconditionally by our Savior and each other. Brothers and sisters were becoming more confident in their walk with Jesus and shared testimonies of the Creator working in their lives. I was blessed and well pleased.

One afternoon there was talk of a stranger in the town near the Rez. My people were always hesitant to allow anyone on or near the Rez—undoubtedly, a result of past experiences. I, on the other hand, became intrigued and took a trip into the neighboring area. With the Holy Spirit's direction, it didn't take long to find this mysterious person. My heart leaped with joy when I saw who was sitting at the café table.

I was overwhelmed with emotions as I ran into the arms of my dear mentor, Mr. Castleman. "How? Why? Here?" I blathered with tears streaming down my face. I was speechless and overcome with emotions. With the calming presence of peace and love that always exuded from Mr. Castleman, I was able to compose myself and, at his request, sat down.

Catching up with old friends is a blessing, but this meeting was beyond words. Mr. Castleman was always about Father God's work, and without hesitation, he began speaking. He prayed daily for all his students, and at times the Holy Spirit gave him insight when one required help. Looking at me with eyes of love and light, he said, "So tell me, how have you been, and what do you need help with?"

I talked all about my journey thus far and that I struggled to help my people move to forgiveness for their own sake. Mr. Castleman was delighted with all I shared and looked like a proud papa sitting there, which made me smile inside. He said I had done well with what knowledge I had so far, and he was there to help me and my people move to fully walk the Jesus way in life.

He then asked whether it would be possible for him to stay on the Rez for a while. However, not wanting to impose or make anyone uncomfortable, he added that whatever the answer was, we could work with it.

That evening at the community meeting, I shared that my dear friend Mr. Castleman was in town. They knew of him because of all the stories I had shared, and to my surprise, they said he could stay as long as he needed. A brother came forward and insisted he bunk with him. I thanked God for the openness and trust seeds that had been planted, for that evening I saw fruit.

Mr. Castleman fit in immediately, and I was grateful. Truthfully, I had no doubts. He joined our weekly meetings and attended Sunday worship, at first just watching, then doing what he was most gifted at: teaching thirsty believers. Our first lesson was about judgment.

Mr. Castleman taught that the Word of God says, "You may think you can condemn such people, but you are just as bad, and you have no excuse! When you say they are wicked and should be punished, you are condemning yourself, for you who judge others do these very same things" (Romans 2:1 NLT).

We need to avoid words that create judgments on God, people, situations, and ourselves. Mr. Castleman shared a few example statements with us.

> I judge if I ... *worry*. Worries are judgments about God; worry implies He can't handle things in your life. Worry edges God out, which is another way of expressing your ego is in control, not God. Prayer and worship carry concerns away.
>
> I judge if I ... *have expectations*. If you have an expectation of others, then there is judgment and control attached. We are to freely give our love, time, gifts, and talents, and not expect anything in return. Yeshua is a perfect example of giving freely.

I judge if I ... *set limitations*. If you are setting restrictions on yourself or other people, you aren't allowing God to do what is best for you and your situation.

I judge if I ... use these terms *if only, can't, should, try, or trying*. These aren't uplifting, encouraging, inspiring phrases; they speak of defeat and judgment before the process has even begun.

I judge if I ... *label things*. We are a society that labels everything, which ultimately results in judgment and discord. As we start to look at life through Jesus's eyes, we will begin to have compassion for ourselves and others. All labels will disappear, and love will remain.

Mr. Castleman said judgments are limiting and the most significant cause of illness. They create hatred, which festers inside your body; disease will surely come, whether it be physical sickness, emotional upsets, addictions, and so forth. Judgment will keep you focused on the wrong thoughts; they will create havoc in your life and prevent you from hearing from God.

He continued, teaching us about words; how we speak creates our futures. He said, "If you don't like where you are in life today, then change your thoughts, which in turn will change your words, which will then change your life. Words are seeds, and they produce fruit. What you focus on will yield the same outcome."

Mr. Castleman then asked us to share what we believed about ourselves. It was evident that we all lived based on our upbringing, environment, and the values our family had taught. This was a difficult conversation, and many became defensive. Mr. Castleman recognized the root cause of our defensiveness as insecurity stemming from beliefs from childhood teachings, people, and situations that had molded our lives.

Mr. Castleman taught that our true identity can be found in the Word of God and who we are in Christ. The good news is that we were made in the image of God; if we are born of Christ, He lives in us. As we study God and His attributes in the Bible and begin to apply them to life, we will become confident and no longer feel the need to defend and explain.

That evening he ended the lesson by teaching on Philippians 4:8–9. " Finally, brethren, whatever things are true, whatever things are noble, whatever things are just, whatever things are pure, whatever things are lovely, whatever things are of good report, if there is any virtue and if there is anything praiseworthy—meditate on these things. The things which you learned and received and heard and saw in me, these do, and the God of peace will be with you."

CHAPTER 8

Reconciliation

Mr. Castleman's lessons continued, and I could feel the peace of Yeshua resting on the Rez, bringing new hope and restoration. My people were thirsty and in awe of this nonjudgmental teaching of the Creator's Son. They learned that the Word says all believers are needed and loved and that we are all uniquely equipped with spiritual gifts.

Every person who walks the Jesus way has at least one gift, dependent on their calling, and sometimes more than one. Believers have a calling and purpose in life, not just as pastors or ministers, as organized religion teaches. Mr. Castleman said, "There are people in your life who will see your words and actions. As you walk the Jesus way in life, lives will be changed, including yours. Through this type of living, you will bring hope to your tribe and surrounding communities."

Mr. Castleman continued, "Brothers and sisters, this is a process and we must be patient." As in the past, he always used active aids with his teachings. We were all excited to learn; for this message, we were making soap. "Soap making," he said, "is a process. Much like all things in this life, it takes patience, perseverance, and more patience."

Our soap-making class was beautiful and filled with many lessons. As Mr. Castleman moved through the soap-making steps, he talked about the connection built through each step to accomplish the end result. In life, as we walk the Jesus way, the end result is to love one another with compassion and a lot of patience. Mr. Castleman said, "Through this type of intentional living, connections and relationships are formed with every step we take, and then we truly live as God intended, helping each other in all things."

Then he said it was time to break down the walls between Christian denominations, between saved and unsaved people, between native and white, and between the labels put on everyone and everything. We needed to focus on the one, Yeshua. Jesus Christ is our example of pure love, forgiveness, and reconciliation—and this is the walk we need to emulate.

Mr. Castleman was excited to share that today there was a great movement that had begun with the goal of reconciliation. He said, "There are many who have realized the injustices done to you and want to gather and apologize. However, you have to lean on the Savior's love inside to be compassionate and open to receiving them for that to happen.

"You are not alone, for Jesus said He would send a helper, a Comforter to help you with your walk on this earth, and His name is the Holy Spirit. He is our comforter, our guide, our small, quiet voice, who is willing to teach and help us through every moment in life. He will guide your every step; He will comfort you in your pain and help you release deep wounds. With His help, you will be open to receiving outsiders onto your reservation to ask for forgiveness."

Mr. Castleman taught us that reconciliation is an instrumental part of healing and restoration in the human race. We can move from past hurts if we follow the teachings of the most remarkable example that walked on this earth, Yeshua. We can overcome. Jesus reconciled us to Creator God when man fell short; we can do this with mankind as we walk by faith.

Pure, honest communication is critical and fundamental for reaching anyone who has been hurt—whether as an individual or an entire nation of people. It is crucial to build relationships and address the past to move beyond it. It will be the grace and mercy of God along with the healing presence of the Holy Spirit that will allow all people of the world to heal.

There will be forgiveness and peace when there is genuine reconciliation through the confession of sin to God and to those who have been offended. However, this won't happen overnight. It will be a progression of humbling steps over time with all parties involved. In time, through this, new relationships will develop. Mr. Castleman ended the evening by asking the crucial question: are you ready to forgive? And I wondered, *Are we prepared to receive people outside our Rez who want to ask for forgiveness?*

To my surprise and without hesitation, my brothers and sisters responded openly, "Yes, we are ready." This indeed was the movement of the Holy Spirit. Never in my lifetime would I have imagined this possible. At that point, Mr. Castleman explained that he knew a group of people he had been working with who truly wanted to move toward healing for the sake of First Nations people and our nation as a whole.

The following weeks were filled with anticipation and a bit of anxiety. We held numerous prayer meetings, knowing that Creator God hears our prayers. We reached out to other tribes and called for a powwow of reconciliation.

Our native powwow represents the circle of life; it's a gathering of relatives of all ages. It allows people to reconnect with old friends and is often where children learn the traditions of their culture. On the day of the powwow, we all dressed in our ceremonial regalia to honor Creator God and our guests. We began the grand entry procession with leaders carrying flags representing each of their respective tribes. They were followed by veterans, who had fought in our wars, then elders, adults, and finally children.

Our honored guests were welcomed as we continued with the beating of the drums and dancing. We shared that for First Nations people, the drum's rhythm represented the beat of the heart. The powwow always reminds us of who we are and renews our spirits, and it is through the drum and dance that we are able to reconnect.

In perfect time, Mr. Castleman proceeded with a ceremony of reconciliation. Our guests gave us a gift, and we reciprocated according to our tradition. Then their representative spoke of the shame and guilt they felt as a people because of their ancestors' actions and the injustices done to such a beautiful people. They sincerely apologized and asked for forgiveness.

In that moment, I anxiously held my breath, awaiting the response of my tribe leader, who stood before them, wondering what would happen. After what seemed like an eternity of silence, she began to speak. She told of Yeshua and walking His way in life, and she graciously accepted their apology. Our guests then presented us with a stone from a piece of land that had been illegally acquired decades ago, which they were now deeding back to us. I was witnessing miraculous healing throughout my people. I peered out across a sea of tear-stained cheeks and smiles of hope I had never seen before—nor will I ever forget. I thanked my God for His hand, for His grace and mercy on us and our guests.

As the powwow ended and our guests left, I eagerly looked for Mr. Castleman to thank him for his help. I couldn't find him anywhere. But instead of panicking like the last time he had left, this time I smiled and rejoiced in the peace I felt. The Holy Spirit assured me that our paths would cross again someday.

I saw a renewed hope and excitement over the next weeks and months among my people. They began to confidently reach out beyond the Rez. They worked alongside non-natives to begin to change the poor living conditions of our people. The Rez finally had clean water and proper electricity. I was humbled, amazed, and blessed by the work Yahweh had done over the year. I knew we were on the road to great healing for my people and the nation.

Personally, it was time for me to move on to the next chapter in my life, though truthfully, I wasn't sure what that would be. One thing I did know was that life is an adventure and a series of journeys. We always have a choice as to which direction we want to take—a path toward hate and strife or a journey to peace, love, and forgiveness.

As I sat there, waiting on the Lord, I heard Yahweh directing me to be still. In my spirit, I heard, "Dwell in the secret place of the Most High" (Psalm 91:1). I was moved to tears as I fondly remembered this was the first scripture I had read with Mr. Castleman. It seemed so long ago, yet the time was fleeting. I thanked God for His faithful servant Mr. Castleman, for the love of Jesus, and for the miraculous healings and breakthroughs.

Father God then instructed me to spend time at a retreat in the mountains to prepare for my next journey. As I communed with Creator God and waited on His directions, I experienced more profound healing to my body, soul, spirit, and a new level of intimacy with Him. I praised Him with hands lifted in gratitude and thanksgiving. I worshipped Him with my drum, rattles, bells, and dance without hesitation as who He created me to be.

God, the creator of the universe, loves me. I have a purpose in my life because of the love of a Savior, Jesus Christ. I am humbled and ever so grateful. I now can love and forgive with the compassion of Jesus. I can now show the world how to live and walk the Jesus way, always giving God the glory now and forever.

I am now ready to begin my next journey to peace wherever He will take me, and what a journey it will be. My name is Shawana. I am blessed and forever God's faithful, loving daughter.

CHAPTER 9

Epilogue—Arise, My People

Billy Graham once referred to the First Nations people as a "sleeping giant." As I was writing this parable, Mr. Graham went home to be with the Lord. He was a great man of God, who touched many lives, and his work lives on today. I see his prophetic words coming to pass as a great awakening has begun among the First Nations people and non-native people alike.

Many native believers are reaching their fellow brothers and sisters, who are hurting, struggling, or lost. They encourage them, helping broken souls heal, breaking down walls, and spreading the truth about Yeshua and His love for all mankind. My website, Journeystopeace.com, lists some of these trailblazers and their websites, social media pages, or both. If you are led by the Lord, please support them to help reach First Nations people and heal our nation.

There is hope for all people, for the world. Jesus Christ, the Way Maker, is the One who will heal, transform through forgiveness, and restore. Laborers are needed; repentance, prayer, and fasting are essential. During this time, a great awakening and revival will flow across the land, and it might possibly be the First Nation people leading the way.

In closing, I want to share with you this love letter I received from Abba as an encouragement for First Nation people:

> My dearest ones, all of you among the tribes of First Nations people who occupied these lands, hear My voice. You have known Me as Creator, walked with Me, learned My ways, and protected My land. The land provided and nourished you. I showed you food to eat, herbs that heal, and warmth. The water was pure, and the earth was green and lush. It is not so today.
>
> There is a great need for revival across this nation, for the land, water, people, and church. Those who caused great harm now need help, and I call upon you as First Nations people to heed the call. For it is only you who know the dire, deplorable state of the earth. You have been beaten, abused, moved from land to land until there wasn't much left for you. We still walk together, but chasms of all the incomprehensible atrocities, plights, and deep hurts have come between us at the hand of the evil one.
>
> I am asking that you would come to intimately know the One who will help you move through your pain and the injustices of the past. That is my Son, Jesus the Christ. For you see, as you come to know Him, you will see the way, the truth, and the life. He is the Savior.
>
> There is an awakening of many of you who are realizing the truth and need to walk the Jesus way. In Him, there is love, compassion, and forgiveness. With Him, you will be able to stand tall, embrace your heritage and your culture, and walk the way I originally intended with Me, My Son, and the Holy Spirit without judgment.
>
> Look to what is coming: a great awakening stemming from a great people. You are needed to lead others across the land with drums, dance, and worship unto Me. You

may have felt as if you were alone, but I have never left you. I need you!

My Son is waiting for you to come to Him as you are, with your regalia, drums, dance, and sweat lodges. Arise, First Nations people; arise and take your stand. Those whom others think are lowly I will use for My greater purpose.

Hear My call. May your powwow be of worship to Me. May your drums beat out to the nations and tribes of this great calling. May your dancing and song be of thanksgiving to My Son. I am Yahweh, and I welcome you into my kingdom just as you are.

Beat the drum and call out to all people. Share the love and compassion of Yeshua through your cultural traditions. Teach of the frailty of creation and the need to heal mankind and the earth.

You are my warriors. Arise, my people!

A PARABLE OF GRACE

Dear Children,

As we go through life, we are faced with many challenges, trials, and tribulations. We make choices daily—ones that bring us peace and others that bring us consequences.

No matter what we are going through, we have a God who understands. We have a Savior, Jesus Christ, who has experienced this human life, and we have a Comforter, the Holy Spirit, who will guide us each step of the way.

Nonetheless, it isn't always that simple, and at times our choices lead us astray. We become lost as sheep who wandered from the shepherd. But be of good cheer; our Father's grace is sufficient.

This parable of grace finds Shawana in a place of peace, but soon trials, illness, pain, and despair test her beliefs before she is ultimately led back to peace. Through Father God's grace, she will have her faith renewed and come to intimately know Yeshua and the Holy Spirit at a deeper level.

May this parable renew your faith and let you know that Abba Father will be waiting for you with open arms no matter how far you stray.

God's blessings and peace ~

CHAPTER 1

Retreat to the Mountains

My name is Shawana. I was born and raised on a reservation in a small community in northern North Dakota, home to the Ojibway people. My journeys to love and forgiveness were transformational, life changing, and I'm ever so grateful to Abba. After my visit back home on the reservation, the Lord spoke to my heart to "be still and seek Him."

Yahweh directed me to a retreat center in North Carolina on Grandfather Mountain, the highest peak of the majestic Blue Ridge Mountains—part of the Appalachian Mountains. The anticipation of what the Lord had stirring brought me a new level of excitement and wonder for this next adventure.

My retreat in the mountains was refreshing, healing, renewing, and enlightening. I have never seen so many beautiful colors—the tranquil blue mountaintops, the lush greenery of the forest, and the vibrant colors of flowers in the flatlands. I was particularly interested in the ground covers; these flowers diligently persevered to grow under the massive trees. Myrtle was one of my favorites with the deep-purple flowers and dark-green leaves, tiny compared to the forest but still thriving. They reminded me of how I sometimes felt small and unimportant, yet I always endured and flourished because of Yeshua.

I loved being surprised each time I came upon a blessing of Father God's creation, be it a small stream flowing with fresh, cold spring water or a dense and fragrant forest that soothed my soul. As I continued to climb, I watched the stream grow into a massive waterfall. My heart leaped with joy at the majesty of creation; it was as if I were continuously sitting in the presence of God in the heavenly realm. As I climbed farther up, the Creators' grandeur could be seen for miles in any direction.

I wondered about animal life, which was active with black bears, cougars, elk, eagles, and so much more. At the top of the summit, I found myself momentarily crippled with sheer panic and fear as I approached the swinging bridge at the top of Grandfather Mountain's peak. Though it was terrifying, the bridge's view was spectacular and beyond anything one could imagine.

I was blessed that Abba chose Grandfather Mountain for my respite as a reminder of my native roots. The Appalachian Mountains on the East Coast are the equivalent of the Rocky Mountains on the West Coast. The Appalachians span from Newfoundland, Canada, to Alabama, United States, consisting of over two thousand miles. The Appalachians are filled with rich Native American history.

Sadly, the first indigenous peoples of the land weren't honored; instead, they were abused and displaced. In fact, the Nantahala Gorge, part of the Appalachians, was included in the Trail of Tears, where the Cherokees were forcibly removed from their homeland; I was heartbroken yet again. Imagining my people's journey from their homeland to Oklahoma and Arkansas reservations was horrifying.

I keep my people's history in my heart, knowing it is part of who I am today, but it is Yahweh whom I lift my eyes to. I must focus on love and forgiveness to continue my walk with Yeshua. When I remember these injustices, I could quickly return to a hateful, unforgiving path. First Nation people have so much to offer. My people's close walk with the Creator from the beginning of time is filled with invaluable insights. I am so grateful that the Creator taught my people how important it is to honor creation, knowing it is our life source.

This brought Mr. Castleman to my remembrance, for he too valued the land. Mr. Castleman was an herbalist; God directed him to study medicinal plants. He took that assignment seriously and shared much of his knowledge with me. I'm so grateful that the topic of medicinal plants opened doors of communication with Mr. Castleman.

I learned about plants I had seen and heard about while growing up on the reservation. Mr. Castleman taught me about the healing properties of plants and showed me how to make tinctures of cinnamon oil, oregano, and so many more. When I was young, I often saw my relatives burn sage during ceremonies. Tribes across the world burned sage in ceremonies for various reasons. Today, as native believers, we use it to purify and remove bacteria from the air, repel insects, and improve our well-being. It also signifies prayers being lifted to Yahweh in heaven.

I also witnessed my elders burning sweetgrass. In the native culture, it represented the Creator and a connection with the earth. Creator God has blessed us with so many different plants for healing the body, soul, and spirit—aloe vera for burns, the inner bark of pines for food, coriander to regulate blood sugar levels, fennel and ginger root for digestive issues, and white willow bark for pain, just to name a few. Mr. Castleman also taught me about essential oils, which are compounds extracted from plants. Some of my favorites are frankincense, lavender, peppermint, lemon, rosemary, tea tree, and oregano.

It has been several years now since I last saw Mr. Castleman on the reservation. I still remember to this day the moment he first walked into my bookshop, Journeys. My life would forever change. Many said Mr. Castleman was eccentric and weird, so they kept their distance from him. I was so accustomed to being different; his mannerisms and odd clothes weren't at all concerning to me.

I vividly remember Mr. Castleman recounting what had led him to my shop that first day. He told me he had been sitting at home in his cabin, reading the Bible, when suddenly God told him to visit the bookstore in town. Knowing it was a Christian bookstore, he hesitated for a moment, wrestling with the thought that he may be judged for being so different from others. Immediately Mr. Castleman cast the thought down, citing 2 Corinthians 10:5. "Casting down arguments and every high thing that exalts itself against the knowledge of God, bringing every thought into captivity to the obedience of Christ."

I fondly remember Mr. Castleman's face and demeanor. It exuded peace, and the sparkle in his eyes was intriguing. He spoke in a loving, compassionate voice as if he knew me intimately; this indeed was the working of the Holy Spirit. We exchanged a few words; he looked around the shop and said he would be back sometime for a visit.

At the time, I was managing Journeys by myself. Sales had been dropping due to massive bookstore chains, so I decided to expand my selection of books. Mrs. Gregory, the previous owner, stocked only Christian books and some small gift items, and that method worked for years. But the competition required me to expand. When I submitted my next inventory order, I selected "spirituality" on the book warehouse ordering sheet. I was amazed at the different types of books that arrived; some excited me, but others I questioned given Mrs. Gregory's values as a Christian.

On one of Mr. Castleman's visits, he noticed some of the different spiritual books. He was loving and compassionate in his questioning, not like some of the born-again Christian women who came in. One woman had threatened me with a book in my face, sternly saying, "You are going to hell for having 'those' books on the shelves." This kind of behavior confused and frightened me; it certainly didn't bring me closer to their Jesus but rather pushed me farther away.

As my conversation continued with Mr. Castleman, I told him one book, *Animal Speak* by Ted Andrews, enticed me as a native person, but fears kept creeping up so I would return it. I did this a few times, and Mr. Castleman roared with laughter—not as judgment but as to how silly we act when we don't understand and live in fear.

My visits continued with Mr. Castleman, sometimes in the shop but usually during hikes on his land. I continued reading books on different spiritual beliefs: Hinduism, Buddhism, New Age, self-help books, and even books on my native spirituality. At the time, I felt this reading was essential in my spiritual walk. I needed to search for myself, dig deep into the different spiritualities, and ponder the "all paths lead to God" view, which was quite popular. I found them all quite interesting, but something was always missing. I couldn't put my finger on it.

One day Mr. Castleman talked to me about the love of Jesus. I was apprehensive and had heard much about Mr. Castleman's God, but I didn't know what to think. As I pondered all that I read, all that Mr. Castleman taught, I realized a few things. I would love to believe that "all paths lead to God" and that everyone would have eternal salvation. However, as I read the Bible, I saw that it clearly stated that to be with the Father, one must come through the Son.

John 14:6 states, "Jesus said to him, 'I am the way, the truth, and the life. No one comes to the Father except through Me.'" All other spiritual beliefs were based on living right and striving to be better through works, reincarnation, earning salvation, karma, and so forth. It was all confusing. I looked at my life and realized I couldn't live up to those expectations in my own right; I am destined to fail inevitably.

The only belief that accounted for my human errors, my sinful nature, was Christianity. In John 19:30, Jesus stated, "It is finished" on the cross. I didn't need to strive, hope, and pray that I would have eternal life—it was promised through Yeshua's shed blood. I still remember the day I received Yeshua as my Savior; it was then that I began living my purposed life.

CHAPTER 2

Refinement in the Fire

So here I am on the mountain retreat, waiting for my next instruction from the Lord. Growing restless, my mind wandered to Mr. Castleman, whom I hadn't heard from since he left the Rez. I decided to settle here in a little town at the mountain base until I had concrete direction from the Lord. I enjoyed meeting some of the local people; they were friendly, laid back, and easy to talk to—something I never would have dared to do in the past.

To fill my time, I began doing beadwork. I had learned this particular skill when I was back home on the Rez before I retreated to the mountains. I found it relaxing, meditative, and healing. In my culture, beadwork is an art form many tribes practice. Differing colors, designs, and patterns identify each of the various tribes. There are two styles, the lazy stitch or the tack-flat stitch. I warmly remembered the wampum made of multiple white and purple quahog shells Mr. Castleman had given me attached to a small pocket knife. I still carry it with me every day.

I decided to purchase a computer and taught myself how to set up a website to begin online sales. To my surprise, my online e-commerce was very successful, and I was often asked to set up a booth at craft fairs to sell my beaded jewelry. I gladly accepted, yearning for companionship and still waiting on the Lord. I realized instantly that many of the people I interacted with believed "all paths lead to God." Confident I was solid in my newfound belief in Yeshua, I thought this was great; I could witness to them.

Over time the opposite began to happen. I listened more and more to the "love walk" they were teaching. I loved Yeshua, but the constant reminder of the enticing New Age views swept me into a world of confusion. I was nurtured and loved by the "Children of Peace," which they called themselves. I finally felt like I had found a loving, caring community of people—a place that accepted me as I was, a First Nation person without judgment.

I was so enthralled by this idea of loving people. At that time, I felt the Lord had directed me to open a nonprofit to teach what I have learned: drumming, beadwork, medicinal herbs, essential oils, and so forth. I drafted a board of directors, and we held numerous events—drumming circles, healing prayers, yoga, dancing under the moonlight during the solstice, and mind-body classes, along with my teachings about medicinal herbs.

The word spread, and people began to come from all directions. Realizing we needed a larger space, I contacted an elderly woman who had once operated a retreat center in the area. I offered to help her maintain the property, now abandoned since it fell victim to vandalism. In return, she allowed us to use the space for some events and meetings. The center once housed a brotherhood of messianic Jewish monks; I thought this would be perfect. I still vividly remember the cross the owner had left at the peak of the roof. I assured myself that this indeed must be the direction I was waiting on the Lord for.

I was stunned as more people came. My heart still belonged to Jesus, but I was actively involved in all the questionable activities and events. We had strong woman groups and took day trips together. I remember hearing the Dalai Lama speak and watching Tibetan monks make a sand mandala at a local college. Their peaceful demeanor was so attractive to me—I yearned for that internal peace.

We held bonfires incorporating sacred ceremonies and invited others to join us. Many people had crystals and gemstones, and claimed they had powers. I remember sitting in a drum circle; I silently offered my prayers to Yeshua and looked around the room, wondering whom the others were praying to. In my spirit, I knew I was being swept into a world of deception and lies, yet I continued.

I became overwhelmed with the number of people involved. I shared with everyone the appeal of "all paths lead to God," careful not to mention Yeshua for fear of judgment. I was ashamed and confused. I was desperate for advice and reached out to a prophet another member wanted me to meet. When I first heard of him, something in my spirit resisted; I was hesitant to talk to him and couldn't explain why. Obviously, my heart knew something I hadn't realized yet. Yet again, that warning in my spirit didn't stop me as my life continued to spiral out of control. After our first connection, I often sought out the prophet's guidance and eventually asked him to move to the area to help. There was no going back; I held the door open for evil to enter.

The prophet moved into the center and began manipulating and controlling people. He instigated issues with board members, and one by one, they left, leaving me to replace them. I started silently watching what was really happening. I increased my prayers to Yahweh, knowing I was now in over my head and in grave trouble. No matter what I did, the prophet verbally accosted and corrected me.

The prophet told everyone that no one but he could hear from the Spirit. By his own admission, the Spirit he spoke of was God, so I thought that wasn't so bad at first. But to say only he could hear certainly wasn't what Mr. Castleman had taught me or what the Bible said. The prophet's knowledge of the Word of God also captivated me. He quoted scripture as well as Mrs. Gregory and Mr. Castleman, so I deduced he must be okay, right? Things only got worse.

I will never forget the night I saw his cat descending the massive staircase; as the cat looked through the rail spindles, I clearly saw a demon in the cat's face. It was at that moment that my eyes were opened. I finally realized that so much of what I was involved in was demonic, filled with deceptions, and I had been targeted to be destroyed. The prophet was here to cause chaos and confusion, and to extinguish the nonprofit. John 10:10 says, "The thief does not come except to steal, and to kill, and to destroy."

I was relieved when the prophet finally moved out of the center into a neighboring house, but he still controlled and manipulated everything from afar. He invited us, the Children of Peace, to his house to perform a cleansing ritual and to pray over his new home. I thought this invitation seemed innocent enough, and I would be safe with the covering of the blood of Jesus over my life. Afterward, everyone gathered in the kitchen; the prophet said, "Someone here is working for evil. The picture of Jesus fell off the wall when she walked into the room, and she needs to be freed."

The prophet then yanked me into the middle of the circle and started accusing me of disloyalty. With tears streaming down my face, my friends, the Children of Peace, gathered around me, quickly forsaking me and blindly agreeing with all the wild, evil accusations the prophet was spewing. In hindsight, I'm sure they were too afraid to speak, fearing they would find themselves the next subject of his wrath.

I loudly cried out to Jesus to save me, and the prophet mocked me, taunting, "You better cry out to Him." I ran to the bathroom, gagging; the evil attack left me physically ill. The prophet followed after me, offering me warm tea to calm me down. When I refused, he forced me to sip it. Before I put my lips to the cup, I silently prayed, "Abba, let not this poison kill me!" As I sipped, the prophet turned away from me to the others, gloating, pleased with his actions. As soon as I had the opportunity, I quickly gathered my things and ran from the house. I was done with all of them.

I was distraught yet grateful I was alive. I repented, cried out to Yahweh, and asked Yeshua for supernatural protection through His shed blood. I renounced and revoked anything spoken over me, did the same for words I had said that led people astray, and blessed them. From that moment on, I locked the center door and refused to answer the phone, though in my spirit, I knew this wasn't over yet.

A few weeks later, a knock came at my door; I saw a familiar and—to my surprise— friendly face. Cautiously, trusting my friend in my spirit, I slowly opened the door. He proceeded to warn me that the Children of Peace were planning a secret meeting to remove me from my position as president of the nonprofit. This was confirmation because I had already gotten that warning in my spirit. I thanked Yahweh for His protection and wisdom.

Sure enough, I was invited to the meeting at one of the Children's homes. I knew I needed to go and did so with the armor of God and the breastplate of righteousness described in Ephesians 6:14. Twelve of them were there, including the board members and others. I felt that this must be what Jesus had endured when He met His disciples at the last supper, knowing He would be betrayed.

The accusations were flying. Most of my charges stemmed from the prophet, who, of course, wasn't there. I recall watching him attack one person after another and wondered when it would be my turn; I guess it was now. His manipulations were pure evil and filled with devious intentions—lies, lies, and more lies.

Satan had accomplished his wicked goal: division, hatred, and destruction. The board of directors wanted me to resign from the nonprofit; I refused boldly responding, "God told me to open this organization, and only God will close it! If you don't like it, you resign." They each quit, scribbling resignations on scraps of paper. I gladly walked out of their lives forever, grateful God had preserved my life.

The betrayal was devastating; I left distraught, profoundly hurt from the treachery, manipulations, disloyalty, and lies. Looking back, I often wonder, *Had I just waited on the Lord as I was supposed to during my mountain retreat, where would I be today?*

CHAPTER 3

Escape to the Hills

I packed my few belongings and found a single-wide trailer to retreat to in the secluded North Carolina hills. My closest neighbors were cows, deer, woodchucks, and birds in the fields, which suited me just fine. I was in the worst emotional state I had ever experienced; bearing in mind the difficulties of growing up on the Rez, I thought that was horrifying.

Over the past year, I felt as though I had completely lost my way. Abba was so distant from me in my heart, but I knew He was faithful as promised in the Word, and He would never forsake me. I dropped to my knees and again asked for forgiveness, repented, and rededicated my life to Yeshua.

For some time, I drifted; my rededication didn't help my frame of mind. I began isolating myself again, appearing only in public when necessary to get groceries, and quickly ran back to the hills as soon as I was able. Again, I didn't belong anywhere, or so I thought. I wallowed in my own world, slowly succumbing to my pain and loneliness.

I was living with relentless apprehensions. Satan and his workers had pulled me into temptation and deceit; I was frozen in fear that the same would happen again if I stepped out. What if I had led people astray again through my ignorance? How would Yahweh ever forgive me if I had done that again?

I had trusted the Children of Peace. At first glance, they had been refreshing. They hadn't been initially judgmental but very loving and accepting of all kinds of people, regardless of race, belief, or sexual orientation. It was beautiful to see this kind of love compared to the judgmental Christians I had encountered. I yearned for that sympathetic, compassionate, nonjudgmental kind of love.

I tried to find Yeshua again in my spirit, but my soul was so cast down. My heart was hardened and so severely bruised that I couldn't be reached, nor was I able or willing to receive. Slowly I settled into life, existing but not living. I continued selling my beadwork online, which sustained me, but life was empty, joyless, and without hope. I thought I just needed time to heal, but I seemed to grow only more downtrodden after months.

One day there was a knock on the door; I was hoping somehow Mr. Castleman had found me. I was sorely disappointed and shocked to see two of the Children of Peace at my door. They wanted to reach out to me and said they'd had no part in the coup attacking me. They continued trying to reassure me that the prophet was a "good man," that my view of him was wrong, and that I should come back. It was the first time in months that righteous indignation rose from my spirit, and I sternly said no.

I shared Yeshua with them. I said, "There was only one I would follow, honor and glorify and that is Creator God, my Father. There is only one I will worship—Yeshua, Son of God. And there is only one whom I will listen to—the Holy Spirit."

Their hearts were hardened, and they didn't have ears to hear; they had been greatly deceived. I silently prayed for them. I was grateful for their visit because I had a small fire lit within my spirit from that point on.

I asked Abba where I should begin my journey back to Him. I clearly heard Him reply, "You do not have a foundation to build on, so start at the very beginning." I immediately started my journey through the Bible; I studied Genesis through Revelation—from the first to the last—and then returned to study the New Testament once again. I had a renewed thirst.

This next season in my life was a time of reflection, meditation in the Word, learning, and listening—which I should have done initially during my retreat to the mountain. The lessons started flowing; lack of patience was my first teaching.

I hadn't waited on the Lord as I was directed; I didn't "remain still." How foolish to think I knew better than Yahweh! I had become self-consumed and lost my focus. I quickly moved from living by my spirit to living entirely in the flesh or, stated another way, the soulish realm. Control, pride, and arrogance aren't characteristics of living a Christlike life. I was so concerned about being liked—yearning for approval and companionship—that I lost all sense of who I was in Christ.

As I dug deeper into the Word, I was stunned to read 2 Corinthians 11:14 in the Bible. "And no wonder! For Satan himself transforms himself into an angel of light." That was it; I had been battling Satan. The prophet was Satan in disguise. Ignorance of the Word had caused me much heartache. Yahweh had given us His Word to live by as an instruction manual, and I had moved without being adequately prepared in life.

The Bible is key to an abundant, peaceful, and love-filled life. The love the Children of Peace displayed was fleeting, not the agape kind of love Father God has for His children. Realizing the love Abba has for me, I looked deeper into what had happened at the retreat center. The prophet had been controlling, manipulative, and verbally abusive. He had ruled with emotional exploitations and threats, and soon physical abuse would have followed. Some people likened it to a cult, which I vehemently denied then, but today I can't help but wonder if they were right.

The Lord showed me that it was understandable that I would fall into this type of relationship. First Nation people struggle daily with identity issues due to circumstances in their lives that are beyond their control. History depicts the removal, annihilation, degrading, and disregard for my people. We are still dealing with this crisis today. Lack of essentials and dreadful poverty drives one to think they are not worthy. I must lift my eyes to the One who created me and stand on Psalm 139:13–14. "For You formed my inward parts; You covered me in my mother's womb. I will praise You, for I am fearfully and wonderfully made; Marvelous are Your works, And that my soul knows very well."

My lessons continued with the Lord; scripture was my refuge. I spent many hours in the Word daily to rebuild my relationship with the Father. I trusted wisdom and revelations would come. I believed I would hear and move with the One who had created me if I devoted quiet time with Him. One afternoon, He was faithful, and I heard this in my spirit.

> Living waters are flowing from My throne filled with life and promises, yet you build blocks, dams—you stop the

flow by looking here, looking there; dwelling everywhere but with Me.

Stop looking outside for approval. Stop questioning; the waters that heal you are deep within. Look to My Son residing within you. His power, His love is right there for your taking.

Go within—not out! Your answers are with My Son deep within you. Be still and let the waters flow. Be still, and you will find the peace you are searching for.

CHAPTER 4

Perseverance

Go within! I now understand what Yeshua was saying, and it will require diligence. I need to consciously pursue God's presence and listen intently to His direction. I walked daily and found peaceful sites to sit at with the Word. One beautiful, sunny afternoon, as I sat next to a flowing stream, feeling the fresh breeze on my face, the Holy Spirit spoke to my heart with a warning. "Perseverance will be critical in this upcoming season. You will experience many things—victories and trials—but must persevere through them all with the Word. Remain focused on My Son. If you waver in your journey, it will be a setback and deter you from My greater purpose."

I didn't quite understand this at the time but knew it was something I needed to keep close to my heart. A few weeks later, I saw an ad in the local newspaper to learn more about historical Christianity; I thought, *Yes, this is the additional preparation I need.* I was careful, though; native people are apprehensive of "Christianity" due to abuse at the hand of Christian ministries, government-run residential schools, and other injustices suffered for religion's sake. I recently read a mass grave had been discovered near an old residential school; there the bodies of over two hundred native children had been found. My heart ached when I read this as tears streamed down my face.

Though still cautious, I was confident the Holy Spirit had brought that ad to my attention; it was time to build a solid basis of knowledge. I completed two online courses called "Foundational Truths." My studies taught me Christian history and explained the origin of the Bible and different translations. The knowledge I gleaned was invaluable, and I was excited to learn more about living an abundant life and walking the Yeshua way.

As the days went by, the Holy Spirit prompted me to continue learning. I decided to enroll in an online program in Christian counseling. I intended it to be strictly for my personal learning and development, but I suspected Father God had further motives. I was finally beginning to feel more confident with this solid biblical foundation, and it was time to venture out into the world again. Little did I know the life lessons that would come from these steps of faith.

Early one morning, Holy Spirit instructed me to check out the Episcopalian church in a neighboring village. It was a small country church; the people were accepting and gracious. I enjoyed the companionship, the hymns, and most especially the choir—it was uplifting and healing for me. At the end of each service, the reverend lit a candle, and the congregation joined hands in a big circle and joyfully sang,

> Flying high on wings of eagles,
> Flying high on wings of love.
> Flying high on wings of eagles,
> With faith, hope, and love.

It was a remarkable image, one I still remember today. I began to engage more and attended the weekly Bible study at the church. The reverend's teaching was informative, but when he instructed us to say, "I'm a sinner; I'm not worthy; I'm no good," red flags immediately went up in my spirit. That's not what the Bible told me. And I had spent too many years considering myself unworthy, controlled, and manipulated by others. What the reverend wanted us to declare just wasn't right. I was amazed by how everyone blindly followed his instructions.

When it was time for group discussions, I raised my hand and gingerly stated that I disagreed with his proclamations. I explained, "Yes, I'm a sinner, but I'm still good. The blood of Yeshua covered my sins. If I sin,

I'm still good and loved; I just need to repent." My message wasn't well received. I knew then that I was done there. I was looking for a place that taught truth from the Word.

Next, at the leading of the Lord, I went to a local community church. It was a larger church, had modern Christian music, lights, and cameras everywhere. At first, the production atmosphere didn't bother me; I joined the worship team and played the congas. The experience brought back the remembrance of my native family and our drumming circles. Not long after I started attending the services, the pastor began showing movies as part of his sermons. The scenes were violent and vulgar; they didn't uplift or feed my spirit. I was shocked these movies had been allowed and thought, *What would Yeshua think of this?* Disturbed, I left—again.

I continued drifting from church to church, searching for fellowship with loving people and deep instruction from the Word. I never wore any of my native clothing, knowing that wouldn't be well received—what a sad thought that was. I attended denominational, nondenominational, Pentecostal, Catholic, and different community churches. Lost and looking for fellowship and additional biblical instruction, I tried it all. The different interpretations of the Bible and rituals fascinated me, but God's presence was always missing for me.

I was saddened when I realized that within the walls of churches sat some of the most "righteous" people I had ever met; this fact was immensely discouraging. Where was the love of Jesus? Who are people to judge which sin is worse than the next? Sin is sin. Alcoholism, fornication, homosexuality, lies, anger, lust—all are sins, yet some people find different types of sin more acceptable. I could never comprehend that logic.

I also realized the dogmatic rules, rituals, and controls created by people were insufficient and unable to sustain me relative to what I found in the Bible and communing with Abba alone. When I was alone with Abba, I had never-ending peace; I just wanted to see this within the body of Christ. I yearned for the love and peace of Yeshua Mr. Castleman shared. I felt as though I didn't belong anywhere.

I was grateful that I had my online studies to preoccupy my thoughts. I walked daily in the hills, thoroughly enjoying the clear, cold-water streams flowing everywhere I turned. The melodies of the birds—especially my personal favorite, the bobolink—lightened my spirits, and together we worshiped the Creator God in song. He would bring my thoughts back to the many adventures I had alongside Mr. Castleman; joy and peace would fall on me.

One day while walking and reflecting, I recalled a valuable lesson Mr. Castleman had taught me. At the time, I hadn't been feeling well and had terrible pain in my lungs, much like when I had pneumonia as an adolescent. Mr. Castleman told me, "Bundle up and go walk up the hill." I thought he was silly; in no way could I get up that steep hill, not in my condition. But he had never led me wrong, so I did as he said. I found a huge tree to sit against and had a long talk with Yahweh. By the time I left, the pain was gone, never to reappear again. We have a good, good Father who loves us. He is waiting with open arms; we just need to draw close and receive from Him.

Occasionally, I reached out to my family back on the Rez. It had been a few years now since I last saw them. I wanted to find myself before I went back. The last time they saw me, I had been filled with love and passion for Yeshua, who overflowed out of me. I had been confident and happy.

But now I was ashamed; I had lost my way. I couldn't let my family see this. What would they think? In addition, now being isolated, I started to observe more negative emotions: anxiety, loneliness, abandonment, self-judgment, and hopelessness.

An unhealthy mental or emotional state eventually manifests physically, which it ultimately did, and illness consumed me. Still intent on finding a place to worship and fellowship, I continued attending different churches as my health allowed. I was surprised by the many Christians who quickly offered reasons for my ailments, telling me, "You must have unresolved sin," "You simply don't have enough faith," or "It must be a demonic or generational curse."

As I continued to struggle with my health, failing to find a congregation to call my own, I knew what I needed to do. God taught us that words create. In Genesis 1 "And He said" was how the earth was formed. I once heard a preacher say, "God is telling us to speak what we need, to confess Scripture over our situations, but we only speak what we see and have." That statement surely convicted me.

Nonetheless, I persevered but failed to thrive as the daughter of the living God. I did confess the Word some days over my problems; other days, I whined and moaned. I spent most of my time living in the flesh, talking about my pain, and being consumed with discouragement. I was indeed confused and lost as a believer.

I still had the nonprofit open. Not knowing what to do with that, I wrote on two pieces of paper, "Keep it open" or "Close it down." I drew weekly until I finally pulled, "Close it down." I was praying for God's guidance, but I was so distant from Him that drawing a piece of paper was the best I could do.

Reflecting, I certainly didn't heed the Holy Spirit's warning to persevere and remain focused on Yeshua. I had the Word, but I was utterly lost.

CHAPTER 5

Tragedy Strikes

The Shepherd will always search for His lost sheep; I am so grateful that He never let go of me through my darkest times. I continued to struggle, knowing a breakthrough was coming; I just never realized that a family tragedy would be the brutal awakening catalyst.

I received a panicked phone call from my family; my sister Aki was missing. Not coming home didn't fit her personality. She was close to our family and had seen the pain a missing or suicidal teenager caused families. Aki would have never put our parents through that torment. They had talked about that possibility in the past, and she had assured them she would never do that.

Aki had been working part-time to help my family with finances. The pay wasn't much, but she'd insisted on doing her part. Her job was about a mile from our home on the Rez, and she walked to work every afternoon and was home by dinner. Her job was during daylight, so my parents agreed it would be okay, especially since the money would be a great help.

Last evening, however, Aki hadn't come home; she might occasionally be late, but she always returned. My parents were frantic, realizing the possible outcome of their missing daughter. It was all too common in our native communities. Across the country, reports of missing First Nation women have become an epidemic. Desperately concerned, I took the next flight out to join my family in the search.

As I sat on the runway, waiting for my flight to take off, I continued my prayers to Yahweh. I silently cried out to Yeshua and to the Holy Spirit to guide the search parties, comfort my parents, and most of all, protect Aki. I called on Yahweh to send ministering angels to assist and expose the evil attempting to take our loved one from us. I rebuked the devil as I had learned in the Bible. My faith prayers were powerful and anointed by the power of the living God within me, but they were fleeting.

I vacillated quickly from one extreme to the next, faith to fear and back again. My fervent prayers calmed me at one point, and I began to research missing and exploited, indigenous women. I was hoping to get insight into what we need to do ourselves, who to contact, and so forth. I was overwhelmed and troubled by what I had read. I read the following in an article of the *LA Times*:

> Last year alone, nearly 5,600 Native American women were reported missing, according to the FBI's National Crime Information Center. The actual number, activists say, is probably much higher, in part because local authorities sometimes mistakenly list the victims as Latina or white. For years, activists and even state officials have acknowledged the inability of tribal officials and local law enforcement to work together to solve them.
>
> Meanwhile, federal studies have shown that in portions of the country with large Native American populations, native women are killed at a rate 10 times higher than the national average.
>
> Consequently, activists have stormed state capitols and flooded social media using #MMIW[9] for "missing and murdered indigenous women" to bring attention to the

---

[9] *Missing and Murdered Indigenous Women*, https://mmiwusa.org/.

violence, which most frequently occurs in parts of the country from rural Alaska to the Oklahoma plains.[10]

I read numerous heartbreaking stories, one after another; most cases didn't end with a reunion of the missing loved one. My anxiety significantly increased, so I paused, breathed, and turned my attention to the promises in the Word. Comforted once again, I continued researching. I learned that the major problem with missing women is coordinating the different law enforcement agencies—state, federal, and tribal. The *New York Times* reported,

> Indigenous activists say that generations of killings and disappearances have been disregarded by law enforcement and lost in bureaucratic gaps concerning which local or federal agencies should investigate.
>
> There is not even a reliable count of how many Native women go missing or are killed each year. Researchers have found that women are often misclassified as Hispanic or Asian or other racial categories on missing-persons forms and that thousands have been left off a federal missing-persons database.
>
> From state capitals to tribal councils to the White House, a grass-roots movement led by activists and victims' families is casting a national spotlight on the disproportionately high rates of violence faced by Indigenous women and girls.[11]

---

[10] Kurtis Lee, *Native Women Are Vanishing Across the U.S. – Inside an Aunt's Desperate Search for her Niece,* https://www.latimes.com/world-nation/story/2020-01-31/murdered-missing-native-american-women, January 30, 2020.
[11] Jack Healy, *An Indian Country, A Crisis of Missing Women. And a New One When They Are Found,* The New York Times, https://www.nytimes.com/2019/12/25/us/native-women-girls-missing.html, December 25, 2019.

Fortunately, there have been new laws passed, such as Savanna's Act,[12] to improve this distressing unfortunate trend of missing women and launch new law enforcement systems to investigate, resolve, and stop crimes against First Nation people. There have also been several social media sites created to bring more exposure to this unseen epidemic.

I pondered the cause of the increased threat to my people, my sisters. Numerous news articles attribute the increase to the oil business on or near native land.

> While the realities facing Native American women and girls are gaining more attention, what is less understood are the effects of extractive industries, mainly oil, on Native American women and communities. Many of the community members I spoke to discussed the influx of crime, sexual violence and drugs when the Bakken oil boom began in 2006.
>
> "Man camps," as they have come to be known, house thousands of temporary oil workers with disposable income, who are dealing with the stressors of dangerous working conditions. Oil industry camps may be impacting domestic violence, dating violence, sexual assault, and stalking in the direct and surrounding communities in which they reside.[13]

Abductions, trafficking, sexual assault, murder, abuse, poverty—how much more must we First Nation people endure? The peace I had by trusting Yeshua when I had started the trip was quickly dissipating with every second. I could hardly breathe, again in a panic, when I thought about Aki.

---

[12] S.227 – Savanna's Act - https://www.congress.gov/bill/116th-congress/senate-bill/227, October 10, 2020.
[13] Sarah Hylton, *A Well of Grief: The Relatives of Murdered Native Women Speak Out*, The Guardian, https://www.theguardian.com/us-news/2020/jan/13/a-well-of-grief-the-relatives-of-murdered-native-women-speak-out, January 13, 2020.

CHAPTER 6

The Ultimate Gift of Grace

My taxi ride to the reservation was agonizing. As soon as I saw my parents, I knew Aki hadn't returned or been found. It had been twenty-four hours since anyone had seen her, and we all knew that as more time passed, the odds of a safe return decreased considerably. All the self-consuming thoughts that had held me captive over the last year instantly seemed irrelevant at this very moment.

I was overwhelmed with concern. Law enforcement on the Rez was still largely lacking; the community immediately started search and rescue teams—so far, no breaks. I tried to pray, but my mind was racing. I decided to take a walk to clear my head, hoping for a miracle. As I rounded the corner near the smoke shop, I froze in my tracks—it was Mr. Castleman!

I ran to him and threw my arms around him, sobbing. Mr. Castleman's peace sheathed me, and I melted as if I were in the arms of Yahweh. As in the past, the Holy Spirit had led Mr. Castleman to me, knowing exactly what was needed. He looked me straight in the eyes and said, "Wipe your tears; we have work to do."

That evening we called a community-wide prayer meeting for anyone not on the search and rescue teams. Mr. Castleman immediately began teaching about the grace of God, the power of community prayer, fasting, and the baptism of the Holy Spirit.

My people on the Rez were overjoyed to see Mr. Castleman again; they warmly remembered him from his last visit. That evening we began with prayer, followed by thanksgiving and praise as we stood collectively on Romans 4:17. "God, who gives life to the dead and calls those things which do not exist as though they did." With one voice, we worshipped Yahweh, thanking Him for Aki's safe return through our tears.

Mr. Castleman then proceeded to teach about God's grace. Yahweh had sent His only begotten Son as payment for mankind's sin—Yeshua is grace. Grace is unearned, unmerited, undeserved, unjustifiable kindness and compassion from a Father who loves His sons and daughters.

To receive God's grace, one must believe in Yeshua as stated in Ephesians 2:8-9. "For by grace you have been saved through faith, and that not of yourselves; it is the gift of God, not of works, let anyone should boast." The Word also teaches, "Let us therefore come boldly to the throne of grace, that we may obtain mercy and find grace to help in time of need" (Hebrews 4:16).

Mr. Castleman continued, "We are in a time of great need, so we boldly approach the throne of God, thank Him for His grace, and plead the blood of Yeshua over our missing daughter. As Yahweh's warriors, we command Satan to take his hands off Aki and return her home unharmed.

"As believers face frightening circumstances, faith can be momentary, affected by what we see and think. In these situations, prayer and fasting are essential to strengthen our belief." "So Jesus said to them, 'Because of your unbelief; for assuredly, I say to you, if you have faith as a mustard seed, you will say to this mountain, "Move from here to there," and it will move; and nothing will be impossible for you. However, this kind does not go out except by prayer and fasting'" (Matthew 17:20–22).

Mr. Castleman told us, "We are not alone; we are never alone—God is with us." He reminded us of his previous teaching that we are spiritual beings with souls and bodies. Our bodies connect with the physical world; our souls are our emotions, minds, and wills. Our spirits are sanctified when we accept Yeshua as Savior. In that instance, the living God, the Holy Spirit, enters our hearts or spirits. Our spirit man is made perfect at that moment and can communicate with God, the Holy Spirit. We can lean on the Holy Spirit for comfort and guidance.

He continued, "For those who so desire with their whole heart, one can earnestly request Yahweh for the gift of speaking in tongues; some call this the 'baptism in tongues.'" Mr. Castleman shared that some believers and denominations don't accept this as a true gift for today, but many do. He shared that he had experienced praying in tongues himself, and doing so had brought him to a new level in his relationship and communion with Yahweh.

Mr. Castleman exhorted us, "It is essential that each son and daughter spend time with Yahweh, not only during a crisis but daily, to build up their spirit. Time with Abba includes reading the Bible, sitting still in His presence, meditating on the Word, listening to teachings online, or attending a church for teachings and fellowship.

"This is not a one-time thing; it needs to be an ongoing process to renew one's mind or soul. Through this communion, one will hear the voice of God in his or her spirit. It is at this particular time that the Holy Spirit will guide you to your purposed life."

We continued to worship Yahweh into the early morning. I was blessed to hear Mr. Castleman teach the truths in God's Word so succinctly within a loving community atmosphere. It was exactly what my spirit was yearning for. Before everyone left, we divided into groups to ensure prayer and fasting continued until Aki came home.

Emotionally exhausted, I went to Aki's room to rest. Instead, I was so distraught thinking about her that I wept uncontrollably. I cried out from deep in my spirit for the Holy Spirit to comfort and help me. I then remembered Mr. Castleman's words regarding praying in tongues.

I thanked Yahweh for the baptism of praying in tongues through my sobbing. Suddenly from the core of my spirit, my sobbing turned into syllables, then words I had never heard before. It sounded like the language of my elders, but it was different.

My tears subsided as I continued to pray in this new and unknown language, knowing in my spirit that Yahweh understood everything I was saying, even if I didn't. Suddenly, a whole new world opened up. I started hearing in my spirit words of guidance from the Holy Spirit.

Walk with Me, talk with Me, and I will show you great and mighty things. Lay down your fears, apprehensions, and doubts, for they are not of Me but of your adversary.

Have you not heard that my Son beat him at the cross? Do you not believe that I will not let you fail or even stub your foot on a stone? My angels have watched over you.

My Son prepared the way; the only obstacle stopping My work from being done is focusing on the wrong thoughts. I have a greater purpose for you, but ultimately it is a choice.

Shall you be concerned over what others may think more than being obedient? You are standing at a crossroad—the wide or narrow path you must choose. I will never forsake you and will continue to love you if you choose the safe way.

But you will never know all that I have planned for you, your purpose will never be fulfilled, and those you could have reached for My kingdom may not have another chance. What shall you say? My people shall perish for lack of knowledge … will you take your place?

    I praised Abba with arms lifted and tears flowing. I thanked Yeshua and the Holy Spirit for love and guidance, for unwavering grace and mercy. I felt peace wash over me. In my spirit, I knew I could now sleep with the wisdom of God in my mind and heart. I could rest knowing that Yahweh was at work in our lives, regardless of the outcomes. Yeshua is the ultimate gift of grace, and His grace is sufficient.

CHAPTER 7

Restoration

I woke with a start that morning. I heard shouts, wailing, and shrieks of joy. I flew out of bed, running through the house and bursting out the front door to see my parents hugging a ragged but alive Aki. I ran into their arms, weeping and overjoyed. As my parents brought Aki into the house, I joined others in the community as we broke out in worship to Yahweh with drums, song, and dance. We danced as David did, glorifying the One and only Yeshua and thanking Him for His grace and answered prayers.

I noticed Mr. Castleman was watching in the distance, exuding the joy and peace of Yeshua as he always did. I waved and smiled with exuberance and gratefulness to him and Yeshua. I was so grateful Mr. Castleman lived the Jesus way. His faithfulness and diligence to follow the leading of the Holy Spirit had blessed us all. I was so excited to share with him all the lessons, trials, and heartaches I had endured since I saw him last. I also wanted to tell him about the gift of praying in tongues and the message the Holy Spirit had given me early this morning. The next time I looked, he had vanished.

I prayed, "Please, Yeshua, let Mr. Castleman remain with us for a while"; however, my spirit knew he had already left. I didn't have time to get distracted by my selfish desires; I needed to see how Aki was doing and what had happened.

When I entered the house, Aki was resting but awake. A family physician stopped by to check her out. It was only by the hand of Yahweh that Aki was well—truly a miracle. Aki shared that she had been walking home from work when a truck pulled alongside her, and she noticed two men in the front seat. Aki knew to keep her distance and quickened her pace. Looking around, she hoped for any sign of life—a house, a vehicle, other pedestrians—but her location was desolate.

While the two men in the cab were distracting her with foolish questions, a third man concealed in the back came up from behind and grabbed her. Aki said she struggled but couldn't break loose. She knew from self-defense courses that the best thing to do was to cooperate until she had an opportune moment to escape. It wasn't until late in the evening that the opportunity presented itself. They stopped for gas; in an instant, she forced her way out of the truck and ran to the woods. The men were in no shape to catch her, so they took off, fearing they might be arrested. From that point on, Aki said she kept a low profile and slowly made her way back home.

The Rez land was so vast that the search parties went in an entirely different location, and Aki had to walk the whole way home. She was familiar with the ground; she knew where water was and munched on some edible plants for strength.

As I listened to her dreadful ordeal, I was grateful for our heritage; she was able to live off the land when needed. As she recounted the events, I also realized that her moment to break free was the same time when we had held the community-wide prayer service. I thanked Yahweh, gave Him praise, and shared this revelation with my family. Yahweh is faithful. The blood of Yeshua had protected Aki from evil intentions, and the Holy Spirit had safely led her home.

Grateful cannot even begin to describe how I felt. My heart broke for all the other abducted native women who hadn't made it back home alive. I must remember to pray daily for the missing women and support #MMIW whenever I can. I'm thankful that others have received a calling from Yahweh to bring this matter to the media's attention. The first step in solving a problem is recognition and acknowledgment.

That evening I sat under the open sky. Everything looked brighter and more full of life, maybe because I finally felt alive within my spirit, once again connected to Yahweh. I spent my quiet time worshipping Yeshua with a small hand water drum I had borrowed from my uncle. Historically, the water drum has been used in native traditions only in spring and summer in a ceremony of forgiveness or thanksgiving after one has beaten the adversary. It brings balance back to life to regain strength mentally, emotionally, and physically.

The water drum is symbolic of the human body, which is roughly 60 percent water. The drum encompasses the four elements: the bottom of the clay pot represents earth; within the drum, there is both water and air; and the maker typically puts a few pieces of charcoal from a firepit inside, representing fire.

My people believe the water drum is a healing drum that restores harmony. After pondering the native traditions of the water drum, I smiled and thanked the Holy Spirit for leading me to select this drum; this was the perfect instrument to sit under the stars with while praising. I drummed unto Yahweh, Creator of all things, thanking Him for beating the enemy and saving Aki. I worshipped Yeshua with all my spirit and soul.

As I sat in Yahweh's presence, I received this message in my spirit:

> O God, when you went out before Your people,
> When You marched through the wilderness, the earth shook (Psalm 68:7).
>
> The heavenly is preparing a people for their marching orders...
> As storms are gathering throughout the earth, we believers know that God had marched before us and paved the way.
>
> When marching orders are released, there will be a great anointing released for those who have a heart for God and are called for His purpose. It will not be done by man but through the anointing laid upon man.
>
> In the natural, there is a need for people to prepare for marching orders. As we prepare, the spiritual realm is in significant conflict, battling to help us prepare.

> Preparation is vital for that which is coming. Meditate day and night in the Word; be obedient to the Holy Spirit's promptings—forgive injustices and move beyond that which is in the flesh.
>
> We are stepping into a time where carnal living and wavering faith will not be sufficient, immaturity will be your downfall, and thoughtless impure, unloving words spoken will create destruction.
>
> Be ever so mindful of these things—be prepared for when Marching Orders are released.

I sat in silence and awe that the Creator of the universe spoke to His children, even today. I had been waiting and yearning for direction. In my spirit, I now understood I had special marching orders designed just for me. I prayed more in the spirit, and the Holy Spirit whispered that I was to go into the world and share with believers and nonbelievers the incomparable gift of grace.

Abba, loving and gracious, had sent His Son to cover all our sins—past, present, and future. Our Father's grace continues as He watches mankind choose malicious actions that destroy people, relationships, and the earth. And Yahweh's grace still endures, even though we turn our faces from Him and His Word.

I must embrace my past and share all my lessons. As a lost, unloved, anxious, fearful, hopeless person, I found the love of a Savior. As an unforgiving bitter, angry soul that was mad at the world, I found forgiveness. As one who strayed far from the love of Father God, I returned to open arms, unconditional love, and never-ending grace.

It will be through sharing my life, trials, and pain that others will understand, and bridges of communication will form; there will be a restoration of hearts. Through my love, words, and actions, people will see Yeshua, the Savior, and be drawn to Him. Barriers will fall, and walls of separation will crumble.

Through these love actions, Satan's lies will be exposed. The identity crisis that both believers and nonbelievers have endured will be defeated, and healing can occur personally and corporately.

These lessons are to be taught in God's creation—in nature watching animals, sitting by water, and breathing the fresh air—so we learn to appreciate and honor the earth before it is too late. As we change our outlook, life becomes an adventure, filled with lessons to grow and become more like Yeshua.

And finally, I am to share with non-natives our belief in Yeshua through the eyes of a First Nation believer. I must help eradicate misconceptions about First Nation people and their spirituality by sharing my cultural traditions.

Immediately, panic began to rise in my soul. I thought, *How will I be able to do this? What do I know? This is beyond my capabilities; why ask me to do this, Yeshua?* Instantly I remembered the time Mr. Castleman had taught me how to capture fearful thoughts according to 2 Corinthians 10:5 (NIV). "We demolish arguments and every pretension that sets itself up against the knowledge of God, and we take captive every thought to make it obedient to Christ."

As I captured these thoughts, suddenly the Comforter brought me back to when I had first met Mr. Castleman, who reminded me of how we took one step at a time. I, too, must take one step of faith at a time. Yahweh is faithful, all powerful, all knowing, and all encompassing. He took me on a journey to peace and restored my heart. I know Yeshua will lead the way for the restoration of all hearts.

To begin this God-ordained journey, the Holy Spirit instructed me that it was time to meet with my elders again. I need to deeply understand my people's spirituality and ceremonies. I praised and thanked the Holy Spirit for guidance, wisdom, and revelations for the glory of Yahweh and the service of His people.

CHAPTER 8

A Great Awakening

I was happy to spend some more time on the Rez with family and elders. I realized I didn't need to stay distant and hide behind my mask of shame when I strayed. That was the evil one manipulating my thoughts and deterring me from my purpose. In Abba's eyes, I was loved, no matter what.

I asked my elders about their view of Creator God. I explained that I had heard a pastor teach that the God our people worship isn't the same as their Christian God. My grandfather explained that people and different religions have many diverse interpretations of the Creator God. He continued, "This is the same for us; some believe native spiritualities are polytheistic, meaning they honor more than one God. While others are devoted to one supreme being, Creator God.

"Now, who has the right to judge if we worship the same God as Christians? It is Yahweh who knows our hearts. When we heard of Yeshua, we rejoiced, for He was predicted centuries ago from our elders that a Savior was coming. Do some First Nation people choose not to believe in Yeshua? Yes, I'm afraid. But again, this is no different than the rest of the world.

"We natives emphasize living in harmony with nature and mankind. We strive to live the way of Yeshua, honoring Yahweh with our cultural ceremonies, respecting others through compassion and understanding. It is a love walk, not a judgmental walk."

I then asked Grandfather about old tribal rituals. "I have heard many say they are pagan, meaning they worship many gods or nature. When I was involved with the Children of Peace, I saw this when they held winter and summer solstice ceremonies, but truthfully, I'm not sure they even knew what they were doing and how dangerous that could be."

Again, Grandfather reiterated, "Yes, some and maybe many were pagan and worshipped nature. I personally did not; I simply knew how important it was to honor Yahweh's creation. We cannot live without the earth, water, and trees that produce oxygen. I cannot speak for all First Nation people the same way you cannot speak for all people, most especially the ones that call themselves Christian."

I was grateful for my elders and blessed with the opportunity to stay at the reservation to observe firsthand First Nation believers worshipping Yahweh. After talking to Grandfather, I concluded that First Nation people are deeply spiritual and have walked closely with Creator God throughout the ages. My people had to depend on hearing His voice to live, to know what to eat on the land, to find clean water, and how to survive in the most dreadful situations. I decided it was futile to determine whether First Nation people honored my Yahweh in the past or whether past cultural traditions were biblically acceptable; this issue was only leading me down a judgmental path.

Instead, I chose to focus on First Nation believers today, their love for Yeshua, and how they meld our culture into honoring and worshipping Yahweh. In doing so, I hope to remove fears and judgments when a First Nation believer enters a church with his or her drum or native clothes. I desire to open people's eyes to the deep spiritual connection we as a people have and embrace what First Nation people have to offer.

The Bible clearly states that we are to worship Yahweh in spirit and truth.

> But the time is coming—it has, in fact, come—when what you're called will not matter and where you go to worship will not matter. "It's who you are and the way you live that count before God. Your worship must engage

your spirit in the pursuit of truth. That's the kind of people the Father is out looking for: those who are simply and honestly themselves before him in their worship. God is sheer being itself—Spirit. Those who worship him must do it out of their very being, their spirits, their true selves, in adoration." (John 4:23–24 MSG)

First Nation believers worship with songs, drums, bells, rattles, sticks, and dance. Hearts are devoted and surrendered to Yeshua to glorify Him with our unique worship. Psalm 149:3 states, "Let them praise His name with the dance; Let them sing praises to Him with the timbrel and harp."

I was convicted. I had let the opinions of others deter and shame me to hide who I was in Christ and suppress my worship style to fit the "norm." As I repented, the Holy Spirit reminded me to lean on the Word of God and remember the lessons Mr. Castleman had taught regarding worship through our instruments. When I set my focus only on Yeshua, I realized that I could worship as the unique person Yahweh had created me to be. This is how all Creator's sons and daughters should live: unashamed of their distinctive, exceptional, and unique qualities and characteristics.

I continued my research and looked further into our traditions and ceremonies, including the sweat lodge, dream catchers, and powwows. I learned that the heart behind the cultural tradition, who is being worshipped and glorified, is significant. The focus needs to be on Creator God and Yeshua; Abba will see our hearts.

Many ignorant people, both believers and nonbelievers, assume our cultural practices are evil without even knowing our hearts. Instead of judgments, diversity should be honored, appreciated, and woven into the body of Christ in unity. This can be achieved only with the love of Yeshua. The agape love of Yahweh needs to be the utmost priority. As we walk in the grace and love of Yeshua, scales will fall from people's eyes.

As I have matured as a believer, I have moved from being concerned about the opinions of others and instead lifted my eyes to Yeshua. I have sung in the spirit, lifting my hands in praise and thanksgiving to Yahweh. I have used my drum to praise Yeshua and awaken my heartbeat of life. I have played my native flute in worship and danced with bells and rattles in pure gratitude and joy to Yeshua. I have used my sticks to break negative thought patterns of my heart and changed my mindset to honor and praise the Creator God with my body, soul, and spirit.

It's time for a great awakening among all people. Transformation is needed within each believer; only then can it overflow into the church as well. The change will occur only if we change our thoughts. To change our thoughts, we need to renew our minds and meditate in the Word day and night.

> My son, give attention to my words;
> Incline your ear to my sayings.
> Do not let them depart from your eyes;
> Keep them in the midst of your heart;
> For they are life to those who find them,
> And health to all their flesh.
> Keep your heart with all diligence,
> For out of it spring the issues of life.
> Put away from you a deceitful mouth,
> And put perverse lips far from you.
> Let your eyes look straight ahead,
> And your eyelids look right before you.
> Ponder the path of your feet,
> And let all your ways be established.
> (Proverbs 4:20–26)

We are to speak the Word of God over life's situations, both personally and corporately, in the body of Christ, also known as the bride of Christ, to receive transformation. There is power in the Word, and it tells us ministering angels are waiting to hear God's Word declared so they can aid in the manifestation of these requests. I immediately imagined how many more prayers would be miraculously answered if we lived by the instructions in God's Word.

Convicted yet again, I realized I still hadn't been diligent in this area of my life. My idle thinking and words have brought my journey to a halt and at times off track. I am so grateful for God's patience and grace.

I knew the wisdom I was receiving in my spirit was life changing. I continued to spend many weeks praying, walking, sitting by waters, and meditating in the Word. I observed God's creation for messages of encouragement, confirmation, and never-ending peace. I chuckled one day as a red squirrel sat perched on a fence post chatting—he had done this many times—and I wondered, *What are you telling me, Lord?* In my spirit, the Holy Spirit reminded me not to let the chatter of unproductive thoughts or people's opinions distract my God-ordained purpose.

God continued to use His creation to remind me He was with me. I hadn't seen an evening grosbeak in years; one day, I quietly asked Abba to bless me with a sighting. On a particularly emotionally challenging day, a flock of evening grosbeaks came to visit and remained with me for a few days. I smiled and thanked the Father. I will treasure that memory as a reminder when I begin to doubt or waver in my faith. I will meditate on the fact that God is faithful, His Word is truth, and He loves me unconditionally.

I remained on the Rez, waiting for the Lord's direction and making sure not to step ahead of His leading. One day in my quiet time, the Holy Spirit startled me when I heard, "Will you be a part of the great awakening coming on the horizon? Will you take your place?"

After sitting in prayer, the Holy Spirit placed on my heart the need to begin an outreach called "Journeys to Peace—The Restoration of Hearts." I was intrigued, excited, and humbled to be part of the Creator's desire to reach His children—those lost and found through love, forgiveness, and grace teachings.

I thought back on all the lessons, trials, and tribulations that had prepared me. First, discovering the love of Yeshua, walking through forgiveness, and realizing the mercy and grace of Yahweh. When I strayed, it was His grace that kept me, His grace that answered our prayers and brought Aki home. I can't begin to imagine life without a loving Father, a Savior who redeems, and a Holy Spirit to guide me daily.

I humbly accepted my God-given purpose from the Holy Spirit to be a vessel, a First Nation warrior. I turn my thoughts only to Creator God. I leave my fears, anxieties, health, and concerns at the altar. I no longer need the "white man" to apologize for the past injustices, so I move forward. I have Yeshua, and He is the way, the truth, and the life for me (John 14:6).

As I share the truth about Yeshua, the Word of God, love, forgiveness, and grace, my prayer is that many will come to know the unconditional love of the Savior. Yeshua accepts us right where we are and loves us just as we are. Cultural traditions don't need to be removed, only incorporated and contextualized to further glorify Yahweh.

Finally, my prayer is that First Nation believers will be recognized, acknowledged, embraced, and instrumental in one of the greatest awakenings known to man. We have walked hand in hand with the Creator God for centuries. We have a deep spiritual relationship with Yahweh and Yeshua, and we have much to offer mankind. Billy Graham once called us the "Sleeping Giants."

"Graham was convinced of God's hand on the lives of indigenous Americans. In 1975, Native Christian leaders gathered to discuss evangelism, discipleship, and church growth among the indigenous peoples of the western hemisphere. Graham said, 'The greatest moments of Native History lie ahead of us if a great spiritual renewal and wakening should take place. The Native American has been a sleeping giant. He is awakening. The original Americans could become the evangelist who will help win America for Christ.'"[14]

One day as I communed with Abba on a hill overlooking the Rez, Aki came running up the slope, excited, waving something in the air. I greeted her with a hug, and off she ran, knowing I treasured my quiet time. Aki had handed me a letter, bewildered by who would write me a note; I opened it.

> My Dearest Beloved,
>
> I am delighted with your growth and know that you are now ready for your most extraordinary assignment in life. Trust that you are well prepared.
>
> Yahweh had known you before you were born. Yeshua has always loved you, and the Holy Spirit will continue to guide you. Ask, and you shall receive what you may

---

[14] Indian Life, New from Across Native North America, *Billy Graham, Who Called Native Americans a "Sleeping Giant," dead at 99*, https://www.newspaper.indianlife.org/story/2018/03/15/news/billy-graham-who-called-native-americans-a-sleeping-giant-dead-at-99/1160.html?m=true, March 16, 2018.

need, but your trust and faith must remain in Yahweh only.

I will be leaving the country to travel worldwide for a season to minister abroad. Enclosed is a key to my cabin. May this be your home base and respite, for you too will soon be traveling for the expansion of God's kingdom.

Now you see clearly with your heart and hear the voice of God in your spirit. It is time for you to speak of the true Yeshua and be as a gentle thunder proclaiming love, forgiveness, and grace throughout the nations.

Step only as Father leads, for He will know the souls that are ready to receive. There will be many restorations of hearts through your love walk; I am excited to see Yahweh glorified and watch a boundless awakening begin throughout the lands.

Walk in your purpose with your head held high, for this is the day, the moment to show the world the grace of Yeshua, the Jesus way to love, forgive, and live.

Step in faith, my beloved, be confident and embrace your new name ...
"Clear Heart – Gentle Thunder."

Fondly and for the glory of Yahweh,
B. C.

Mr. Castleman—I was stunned! What a blessing to move back to New Hampshire and live in such an anointed abode. I was beyond excited to see the beautiful cabin nestled in the woods again. I was looking forward to the moment I stepped onto that wooden bridge, feeling the water splash onto my feet as it had years ago, symbolizing my new beginning and taking my mantle into the world.

I still wish Mr. Castleman was here to help me begin this outreach, but I know in my heart this is my journey with Yeshua. One day our paths will cross again if not here on earth, most assuredly in heaven. For now, I must be about my Father's business.

As I begin this new adventure, I now know who I am in Christ. I am a First Nation believer who walks the Jesus way. I stand on the promise in the Word: "I can do all things through Christ who strengthens me" (Philippians 4:13).

I am Shawana, "Clear Heart—Gentle Thunder," a First Nation warrior for Yeshua, spreading love, forgiveness, and grace throughout the lands.

CHAPTER 9

Epilogue—Will You Be Ready?

Change is constant, but God is never changing; He is always faithful and ever with us. Grace is undeserved favor through Yeshua. It is only by and through His grace that believers can live an abundant, blessed life, knowing God's grace is sufficient no matter the situation or what the future holds.

The Word of God teaches dangerous times are coming and will increase as we approach the end of this dispensation. "But know this, that in the last days perilous times will come: For men will be lovers of themselves, lovers of money, boasters, proud, blasphemers, disobedient to parents, unthankful, unholy, unloving, unforgiving, slanderers, without self-control, brutal, despisers of good, traitors, headstrong, haughty, lovers of pleasure rather than lovers of God, having a form of godliness but denying its power. And from such people turn away!" (2 Timothy 3:1–5).

We are in a time of many trials these days; 2020 brought into our world a pandemic like one has never seen before. There has been political unrest, censorship, riots, anger, and fear that has captured the hearts of many. People are frantically looking for answers amid chaos and facing an unknown future. It's time to turn back to the Bible, back to our roots. There is one who saves and helps us navigate the turmoil in the world, and that is Yeshua. When you choose Jesus, you choose life.

Be alert and aware; in the meantime, the world needs healing. People need healing in their bodies, souls, and spirits. The church must return to Yeshua. The restoration of hearts will require laborers, believers walking the way of Jesus in love, humility, and compassion.

Presently, there is a remnant of people, including First Nation people, praying, fasting, and working diligently for the kingdom. Anticipation is building; a spirit of revival has been stirring and has grown rapidly over this last year. Many believers have turned their face to Yahweh, have stopped living a carnal life, and choose to walk in the Spirit daily.

In the last days, Yahweh will speak to those who have ears to hear more than ever.

> And it shall come to pass in the last days, says God,
> That I will pour out of My Spirit on all flesh;
> Your sons and your daughters shall prophesy,
> Your young men shall see visions,
> Your old men shall dream dreams.
> And on My menservants and on My maidservants
> I will pour out My Spirit in those days;
> And they shall prophesy.
> I will show wonders in heaven above
> And signs in the earth beneath:
> Blood and fire and vapor of smoke.
> The sun shall be turned into darkness,
> And the moon into blood,
> Before the coming of the great and awesome day of the Lord.
> And it shall come to pass
> That whoever calls on the name of the Lord
> Shall be saved.
> (Acts 2:17–21)

Restoration is upon us. Change is unquestionably coming. Will you be ready? This is a word the Holy Spirit revealed to me a few years ago; I pray it blesses you.

> The winds of change will fall on the earth, and only those who trust Me and stand on My Word will be able to withstand and lead others.
>
> It will be a supernatural time filled with miraculous wonders and healings by My Hand, and by the powers of evil lurking—discern the difference. Stay close to Me as I go before you.
>
> It will be a wonderful time and a time of great fear for those who do not know Me. Draw close, remain faithful, and *My* grace will be sufficient for You.
>
> Be in the Spirit, pray in the Spirit, and you will know when your marching orders are released. Do not look to your neighbor, for your time will be different from his time, from her time.
>
> Be about My business, keep your focus on My Son and the way He fulfilled His purpose for Me. There will be no time more significant on the earth except when My Son took your sins on the cross.
>
> A new kingdom is coming, one that will glorify all that is good and destroy evil. Blood will be spilled, or the blood of My Son will save. The earth will be cleansed by the blood.
>
> Patience is vital; timing is essential. Marching orders will be coming for those who have ears to hear. My remnant is preparing. Anointed marching orders will begin, and some places have already started.

Do not move by the flesh, only by what is spoken to you in your spirit by My Spirit. Since creation began, I Am has gone before you. End times will be no different.

Be still and know My voice.

Worship in prayer, fasting, song, and dance. Worship creates the power from the heavens to fall on you. Dance gives you the strength to be My warrior, and the drum will beat out marching orders throughout the spiritual and natural realm.

Will you be listening?

Will you be ready?

BIBLIOGRAPHY

Alexander, Corky. *Native American Pentecost—Praxis, Contextualization, Transformation.* Cleveland, TN: Cherohala Press, 2012.

Arrien, Angeles. *The Four-Fold Way – Walking the Paths of the Warrior, Teacher, Healer and Visionary.* New York: HarperCollins, 1993.

Congress.gov, *S.227 – Savanna's Act,* Bill passed, October 10, 2020. https://www.congress.gov/bill/116th-congress/senate-bill/227.

Garfield, Jonathan, Indian Country Today Network, *A Thanksgiving Poem by Jonathan Garfield,* https://newsmaven.io/indiancountrytoday/archive/thanksgiving-a-poem-by-jonathan-garfield-hHK2ksuqskKKLO8spK8SSw/, November 28, 2013.

Hayford, Jack W. *The New Spirit Filled Bible, NKJ,* Nashville, TN: Thomas Nelson, Inc., 2002.

Healy, Jack, The New York Times, *An Indian Country, A Crisis of Missing Women, And a New One When They Are Found,* https://www.nytimes.com/2019/12/25/us/native-women-girls-missing.html, December 25, 2019.

Hylton, Sarah, The Guardian, *A Well of Grief: The Relatives of Murdered Native Women Speak Out.* https://www.theguardian.com/us-news/2020/jan/13/a-well-of-grief-the-relatives-of-murdered-native-women-speak-out, January 13, 2020.

Indian Life, News From Across Native North America, *Billy Graham, Who Called Native Americans a "Sleeping Giant, Dead at 99.* <u>https://www.newspaper.indianlife.org/story/2018/03/15/news/billy-graham-who-called-native-americans-a-sleeping-giant-dead-at-99/1160.html?m=true</u>, March 16, 2018.

Janko, Melinda, dir. *100 Years; One Woman's Fight For Justice.* Fire Belly Productions, Inc. 2016. Aired March 20, 2018 – March 20, 2020, on NETFLIX. <u>https://www.100yearsthemovie.com/</u>.

Lee, Kurtis, The LA Times, *Native Women Are Vanishing Across the U.S. – Inside an Aunt's Desperate Search for Her Niece,* <u>https://www.latimes.com/world-nation/story/2020-01-31/murdered-missing-native-american-women</u>, January 30, 2020.

Missing and Murdered Indigenous Women USA, <u>https://mmiwusa.org/</u>

Wilson, James. *The Earth Shall Weep, A History of Native America.* New York, NY: Grove Press, 1999.

AFTERWORD

Journeys to Peace: Parables of Love, Forgiveness, and Grace was created from a unique blend of personal experiences and facts initially used for my master's thesis on "First Nations People—Past, Present, and Future." The paper captured historical facts of Native American people and the injustices they experienced in the past and continue to endure today.

Witnessing how deeply moved my professor, also part native, was while reading the thesis, I was intrigued by the thought of publishing the paper as she suggested but recognized it wasn't an enjoyable read in its current state. Through praying and waiting on the Lord, *Journeys to Peace* was planted in my heart with the desire to tell this God-inspired story to promote healing through Jesus Christ for an individual, First Nation people, and our nation.

Journeys to Peace was written with the Holy Spirit's guidance as a collection of parables intended to take the reader on a visual journey and teach about the love of a Savior and the power of forgiveness. It was initially published without "A Parable of Grace." Deep in my spirit, I felt something was missing, and the Holy Spirit showed me a life of love and forgiveness isn't complete without grace.

The first two parables were updated, and *Journeys to Peace* was republished with the addition of the grace parable. It is based on a fictional character but incorporates many personal life lessons from a special friend, much like Mr. Castleman. Our adventures were great fun though sometimes challenging and life changing. Nevertheless, all were powerful teaching tools.

In addition, my friend introduced me to people from the Oneida

Indian Nation Tribe. Personally, I witnessed the heartache that continues to keep them and their native brothers and sisters in bondage today. The mission of this book is to bring attention to the injustices and hardships First Nation people endure today. Poverty, suicide, addiction, depression, lack of human necessities, unemployment, and now the threat of missing indigenous women in reservations all need to be exposed and brought to our nation's consideration.

As I move forward in my next God-ordained assignment, I will be exploring the restoration of man's heart for both native and non-native people. I hope to enlighten non-native people by resolving misconceptions about First Nation believers by sharing what I have learned. I believe once you hear stories from First Nation people, their love for Jesus, their forms of worship, the body of Christ will understand and experience the joy of praising God with new freedom and love for one another.

I am excited to see where this next journey takes us; together we can grow, learn to walk in a deeper relationship with Yahweh, and live the Jesus way. Please check out my website, Journeystopeace.com, for further information.

As for now, I pray these parables encouraged you, touched your soul, and brought you to a place of peace as they have for me in my life.

I pray you will walk with Yahweh daily, meditate on His Word, and know you are loved by the Creator God, Yeshua, and the Holy Spirit.

You are unique, you are needed, and you have a God-given purpose in your life. I pray Yahweh will always protect you, direct your every step, and give you the desires of your heart.

May all your journeys be journeys to peace.

God's blessings and peace ~

tr

LET ALL THINGS PRAISE HIM

Praise God in His sanctuary;
Praise Him in His mighty firmament!
Praise Him for His mighty acts;
Praise Him according to His excellent greatness!
Praise Him with the sound of the trumpet;
Praise Him with the lute and harp!
Praise Him with the timbrel and dance;
Praise Him with stringed instruments and flutes!
Praise Him with loud cymbals;
Praise Him with clashing cymbals!
Let everything that has breath praise the LORD.
Praise the LORD!
(Psalm 150)

ABOUT THE AUTHOR

TR Brennan earned a master's degree of Ministry in Christian counseling from International Seminary in Florida, and a doctorate of Ministry from Newburgh Theological Seminary in Indiana.

With a God-given heart for Native Americans, she is empathetic to the plight of all First Nations people. Her heart's desire is to bring awareness to their history and the issues they endure today. Her goal is to awaken non-natives to common misconceptions regarding First Nation people's spirituality and their walk with Creator God, and to encourage others to embrace native believers who walk the Jesus way in life. She believes that healing individually and collectively will lead to the healing of our nation.

Her passion is writing and helping people find their path to abundant life by speaking the Word and appreciating God's creation. She resides in Upstate New York with her husband; their dog, Sarabi; and their cat, Isaiah, on fourteen acres they call the "Promised Land." They like to sit by water, hike, kayak, and walk the land, observing all of God's creation and relishing all His blessings.

The Oneida Nation, People of the Standing Stone of the Haudenosaunee, are the indigenous peoples on whose ancestral lands we gratefully reside.